MEET THE
Silver Blades Skaters . . .

Nikki, Tori, Jill, Haley, Amber, and Martina are six talented skaters who share one special dream— competing in the Olympics someday. And they're going to try to make it all happen in Silver Blades, the best skating club around!

RIVAL ROOMMATES

Jill can't believe it! Her new roommate at the Ice Academy is Carla Benson—an old rival from another skating club.

Carla loves to win, and she's determined to beat Jill at *everything*. Whatever Jill does, Carla tries to do it just a little bit better. Whether it's clothes or grades or figure skating, Carla and Jill are constantly competing at something. Jill enjoys the challenge of their *un*friendly competition on the ice. But then Carla goes one step too far. Can Jill stop Carla from stealing her new boyfriend, Josh?

Don't miss the ON THE EDGE, Book One in the Silver Blades Gold Medal Dreams trilogy.

US $3.50 / $4.75 CAN
ISBN 0-553-48511-3
48511

0 76783 00350 7

S

A SKYLARK BOOK
New York
RL: 5.0
009–012

Have you read these Silver Blades books?

BREAKING THE ICE
IN THE SPOTLIGHT
THE COMPETITION
GOING FOR THE GOLD
THE PERFECT PAIR
SKATING CAMP
THE ICE PRINCESS
RUMORS AT THE RINK
SPRING BREAK
CENTER ICE
A SURPRISE TWIST
THE WINNING SPIRIT
THE BIG AUDITION
NUTCRACKER ON ICE
RINKSIDE ROMANCE
A NEW MOVE
ICE MAGIC
A LEAP AHEAD
MORE THAN FRIENDS
WEDDING SECRETS
NATALIA COMES TO AMERICA
THE ONLY WAY TO WIN
RIVAL ROOMMATES

JILL SMELLS A RAT

Jill woke with a start. Something was wrong! The room was way too bright for early morning. She glanced at her alarm clock. Eight A.M.! Her stomach lurched. She had overslept by two hours!

Jill threw off her covers and jumped up. Carla's bed was empty and her skate bag was gone. As Jill rushed around the room, throwing on clothes and grabbing her school things, she tried to figure out why her new alarm clock hadn't worked.

She pictured herself switching her stuff with Carla's the night before. She *knew* she had moved her clock to her desk, plugged it in, and set the alarm. She knew because it had been flashing 12:00 and she'd double-checked the instructions before she reset the clock and turned the alarm on.

Jill stopped and looked at the black plastic clock. The alarm button was set to OFF. And on top of the button was a thick, greasy smudge. Jill wiped her finger over the smudge. It felt like hand cream. She held her hand under her nose and smelled a sharp orange scent—that was the scent of the cream Carla used every day!

RIVAL ROOMMATES

Melissa Lowell

Created by Parachute Press, Inc.

A SKYLARK BOOK
NEW YORK · TORONTO · LONDON · SYDNEY · AUCKLAND

With special thanks to Darlene Parent and
Sky Rink Skating School, New York City

RL 5.2, 009–012

RIVAL ROOMMATES
A Skylark Book / September 1997

Skylark Books is a registered trademark of Bantam Books,
a division of Bantam Doubleday Dell Publishing Group, Inc.
Registered in U.S. Patent and Trademark Office and elsewhere.

Silver Blades® is a registered trademark of Parachute Press, Inc.
The logos of the United States Figure Skating Association
("USFSA") are the property of USFSA and used herein by
permission of USFSA. All other rights reserved by USFSA. USFSA
assumes no responsibility for the contents of this book.

Series design: Barbara Berger

ISBN 0-553-48511-3

Published simultaneously in the United States and Canada

Bantam Books are published by Bantam Books, a division of
Bantam Doubleday Dell Publishing Group, Inc. Its trademark,
consisting of the words "Bantam Books" and the portrayal of a
rooster, is Registered in the U.S. Patent and Trademark Office and in
other countries. Marca Registrada. Bantam Books, 1540 Broadway,
New York, New York 10036.

PRINTED IN THE UNITED STATES OF AMERICA

OPM   0 9 8 7 6 5 4 3 2 1

1

"**H**ey, Jill, watch out!"

Jill Wong turned just in time to see a snowball flying straight at her. She ducked and the snowball whizzed over her head, leaving a dusting of white on her shiny black hair.

"Jesse! I'm going to get you!" she cried.

Jill threw down her skate bag and quickly packed a huge snowball. She hurled it at Jesse Barrow. The cold, wet snow hit him right in the chest.

"Ohhh, you got me!" Jesse clutched his heart and fell backward into the snow. Jill giggled and ran over, flopping onto her knees beside him.

"You'll have to go on without me, Jill," Jesse whispered. "Think of me while you're skating at Sectionals. Win the gold . . . for me." He gurgled and then lay still.

"Please don't leave me!" Jill said, giggling again. "I know! Maybe some snow down your neck will revive you!" She quickly scooped up a handful of snow and tugged at Jesse's scarf.

"No!" Jesse laughed and grabbed Jill's hands.

Jill looked into Jesse's sparkling gray eyes. The smile faded from his face. He sat up, but he didn't let go of her hands.

"Jill," he said. "Listen, I—"

"Hi, you guys!" called a loud voice. Jesse quickly dropped Jill's hands, and they both looked up. Their friend Bridget Harris was scurrying down the walkway from the International Ice Academy's skating arena. "See you in the dining hall later tonight!" she called as she passed them.

"Okay, see you later," Jesse said. He stood and offered Jill a hand, pulling her to her feet.

Jesse was fifteen, a year older than Jill. They had been friends since Jill had been accepted at the International Ice Academy in Denver about a year earlier. The prestigious school had only thirty students—eighteen boys and twelve girls.

Jill saw Jesse every day, and they'd been close friends for a while. But lately Jill also had a big crush on Jesse. For the past week, Jill had been hoping that he would ask her to the Academy's formal dance. She could just picture how handsome Jesse would look in a dark suit and tie. Jill was almost sure Jesse had been about to ask her to the dance when Bridget walked by. But now it seemed as if the moment had passed.

"Hey, you looked great in practice today," Jesse said. He brushed some snow off his down jacket and pushed his blond hair off his forehead. "Your triple toe loop combination was awesome."

"Thanks. It's part of my new routine for Sectionals," Jill answered. She picked up her skate bag, and they started down the walkway. For a minute they strolled in silence. Their breath made clouds in the cold air. In the distance, the sun was setting over Colorado's Rocky Mountains.

The campus at the Academy looked extra beautiful with all the snow on the ground, Jill thought.

As they walked by a lamppost, the light clicked on.

"Wow, it's getting dark really early these days," Jesse said. He looked at his watch. "It's only five o'clock."

"Five!" Jill gasped. "Oh, no—I've got to hurry. Bronya's leaving for Switzerland any minute! I have to say good-bye."

Bronya Comaneau was Jill's roommate at Aspen House, the girls' dorm. They had shared a room since Jill had gotten into the Academy.

"Again? Haven't you two said good-bye about a hundred times already?" Jesse teased. "Hey, I'll go with you. I want to say good-bye, too."

They started jogging toward the big old house.

"So where's Bronya going, again?" Jesse asked, puffing.

"Jesse! I've told you about a million times!" Jill laughed. "It's a huge new rink in Geneva. Bronya's old coach from Romania is running it. She's really psyched about working with him again."

A minute later, they dashed onto the porch of Aspen House. Jesse pulled open the big wooden door.

"Come on." Jill led Jesse through the dorm's common room and up the stairs. They bounded down the hall and burst into Jill's room.

"Hey! Where's the fire?" Bronya turned from her bed. "You two scared me!" She sat down next to the huge blue suitcase she had been struggling to close. It was almost as big as Bronya. She was a petite girl with light brown hair tucked back in a bun.

"Sorry, Bronya," Jill said. "We were afraid we were going to miss you. When is the taxi coming to take you to the airport?"

"At quarter to six," Bronya said in her heavy Romanian accent. "But I will never make it if I cannot close this." She gestured at the suitcase, which was overflowing with clothes.

Jill giggled. "I guess that means you'll just have to stay here in Denver with us."

"I don't think so," Bronya said. "Maybe I'll just take less stuff with me." She reached quickly into the suitcase and grabbed a soft pink angora sweater. "Here, Jill, you keep this."

"No way, Bronya," Jill protested. "That's one of your favorite sweaters."

"Go ahead, Jill," Bronya insisted. "I know you always liked this one—I know because you borrowed it so much! It looks really good on you."

Jill hugged the sweater to her chest. "I'll think of you every time I wear it. Thanks, Bronya," she said quietly.

"It's nothing," Bronya said. Bronya's eyes became teary. She turned away and yanked at the zipper on the suitcase.

"Remember," Bronya said, clearing her throat, "you promised to write me and tell me everything that happens here."

"I will," Jill said. She felt a tear slip down her cheek and she wiped it away quickly. "Hey, we'll be seeing each other on the ice again."

"I know," Bronya agreed.

"At the Olympics!" they said at the same moment. Both girls started giggling.

Jesse shook his head. "Crying one minute and laughing the next. What is it with girls?"

Bronya looked at him. "Believe me, boys don't always make much sense, either. Girls show what they feel. But boys hold everything in. Sometimes they are even too shy to ask certain questions." She turned to Jill. *"Right, Jill?"*

Jill's face grew hot. "Bronya!" Jill said, poking her.

"Ouch!" Bronya squealed. "Questions about things like *dances*," Bronya continued. Jill cringed. Bronya knew Jill wanted to go to the Academy's formal dance with Jesse. Now Bronya was dropping hints to him!

"Oh, this reminds me that the dance is in three weeks," Bronya went on. "I'm sad that I will miss it. Are you going to the dance, Jesse?"

"I guess so." Jesse shrugged.

"And, Jill, are you go—"

Jill couldn't stand any more. *"Bronya!"*

Jesse and Bronya both turned to her.

"Let's get your suitcase closed!" Jill said, pressing down hard on the overstuffed bag. She leaned over the suitcase so Jesse wouldn't see how red her face was.

"Let me help," Jesse said, stepping beside Jill. "What this job calls for is guy power." He pushed down hard on the suitcase. As he did, his hand grazed Jill's. He glanced at her and smiled shyly. Jill smiled back.

Suddenly, the suitcase slipped off the bed and onto the floor, spilling Bronya's clothes everywhere.

"Guy power, eh?" Bronya mocked.

Jesse looked sheepish. "Sorry about that. Here, I'll help you pick your stuff up."

"That's okay," Bronya answered. "Maybe you could be nice enough to use your guy power to carry down my other suitcases?"

"Okay, sure," Jesse said. He grabbed the two red cases next to Bronya's bed and dashed out of the room.

The second he left, Jill turned to Bronya. "I can't believe you said all that stuff about the formal!"

Bronya grinned. "Pretty good, huh?"

"It *was* funny," Jill admitted. "But I'm not sure he got the hint."

Jill sat down on the bed and sighed. "Maybe he doesn't want to go with me to the dance."

"Of course he wants to go with you," Bronya almost shouted. "Anyone can see that!"

"I hope you're right," Jill said. "I think he was just about to ask me today, but then he didn't."

"Maybe he's too shy. Maybe you should just ask him," Bronya suggested.

"I guess I could," Jill agreed. "But that's kind of scary!"

"That's probably exactly how Jesse feels," Bronya pointed out. "Now help me carry the rest of this stuff downstairs."

Jill grabbed Bronya's skate bag. Bronya picked up the big blue suitcase, and they walked to the door. Bronya turned and looked back at the room. She gazed out the picture window at the snow-covered mountains glowing in the twilight.

"I'm going to miss this place," she said. "And I'm going to miss you so much, Jill. You're one of the best friends I ever had."

Both girls put down their cases and gave each other a tight hug.

"Oh, Bronya. Who's going to give me advice and plan my life?" Jill asked. "What am I going to do without you?"

"You're going to do what you always do—keep taking my advice," Bronya said, giggling. "Only now you will take it over the phone and in letters!"

The two girls walked downstairs and out to the driveway, where Jesse was waiting. Minutes later, the cab pulled up. They loaded Bronya's things into the trunk. As the car pulled away, Jesse and Jill waved good-bye. Bronya waved back until the taxi turned onto the main road and pulled out of sight.

Jill turned to Jesse and sighed. "I miss Bronya already."

Jesse squeezed Jill's arm. "Well, my Romanian accent is a little rusty, and I look really, really bad in a skating dress. But if you want, I'll pretend I'm Bronya," he said. "Only until your new roommate gets here, though."

"*Jesse!*" Jill said, punching him lightly in the arm. "In that case, let's hope my new roommate gets here *soon!*"

2

Jill rushed into the arena the next morning. She was late for seven A.M. practice.

She ran through the huge lobby into the girls' locker room. It was empty! Everyone else was already on the ice.

Jill yanked off her boots and pulled on her skates, tying them quickly. Then she raced to the rink. Ludmila Petrova, Jill's coach, was standing in the center.

"Young lady! You're late!" Ludmila shouted in her heavy Russian accent. "Would you care to explain?"

Ludmila had been a top Russian skater many years ago. Now she owned the Academy with Simon Wells, a former ice dancer. She also taught many of the students. She was a strict coach—very strict.

A couple of other skaters glanced over to see whom

Ludmila was yelling at. Jill blushed as she yanked off her skate guards and stepped onto the ice.

"Sorry, Ludmila," Jill said, gliding up to her coach. "Bronya left yesterday. Her alarm clock always woke me up. Without it I overslept."

Ludmila narrowed her brown eyes and shook her head. "No good, Jill," she said.

"But Ludmila—my alarm clock's broken, and I just forgot that Bronya packed her cl—"

"Jill!" Ludmila cut her off. "Do you think that excuse makes your double axel higher? Or your sit spin tighter?"

"No," Jill said, looking down at the ice.

"This Academy has thirty students," Ludmila continued. "The waiting list has more than one hundred names on it. Names of some of the most promising skaters in the world. They will be glad to come take your place here—and I am certain they will show up to practice on time. Is that clear?"

"Yes, Ludmila," Jill mumbled, trying not to cry. Out of the corner of her eye, she saw that several skaters had slowed down and were listening to Ludmila's lecture. She prayed Jesse wasn't in earshot. Jill wanted to sink into the ice and disappear.

"One last thing, Jill," Ludmila said more gently. "You are here for yourself. So that means you rely on yourself. You compete with yourself. You skate for yourself. And you buy yourself an alarm clock, okay?"

Jill nodded. She looked up and saw that Ludmila was smiling. "Let's get to work. Sectionals are only two weeks away. And you've already missed fifteen minutes of practice."

"There," Jill said out loud, pushing the last thumbtack into her favorite Kristi Yamaguchi poster. She stood back and studied the results. "Perfect!"

Jill had left dinner early and returned to Aspen House. Then she had moved all her things over to Bronya's side of the room. The bed was closer to the window, the dresser was bigger, and the desk had an extra drawer. She had pinned the poster right over her new desk.

There was a knock at the door. "Phone call, Jill!" a girl's voice called out.

"Okay, thanks." Jill hurried into the hall and picked up the phone. "Hello?"

"Hi, Jill!" a voice said over the line. "Guess who!"

"Tori! Hi!" Jill said. Tori Carsen was one of her closest friends from her old skating club in Pennsylvania, Silver Blades.

"Guess again!" This time the voice sounded completely different.

"Haley?" Jill said, puzzled. "At first you sounded exactly like Tori." Haley Arthur was another of Jill's good friends from Silver Blades.

"Guess again!" Now the voice sounded like Nikki Simon's. She also belonged to the club.

"Nikki? What's going on?" Jill said. There was muffled laughter on the other end.

"It's *all* of us!" the three friends said together.

"It's a conference call!" Tori said excitedly. "My mother got a new phone system for her fashion-design business! Now we can all call you at once."

"Awesome!" Jill exclaimed. "How are you guys? I miss you so much! Bronya left tonight and I'm all alone!"

"We miss you, too," Haley said. "How's the Academy?"

"Yeah, how's everything going with Jesse?" Tori asked.

"Okay, I guess," Jill answered. "But he didn't ask me to the dance yet."

"He didn't?" Tori said. "When is that dance, anyway?"

"Three weeks," Jill said. "I keep thinking he's about to ask . . . but he never does. I don't know what to do."

"I know what to do," Tori said.

"Really? What?" Jill asked eagerly.

"Get Veronica on the phone!" Tori answered. Veronica's father, Roger, was married to Tori's mother. Veronica had shown up to visit Roger one day and ended up moving in with him, Tori's mom, and Tori.

At fifteen, Veronica was only a year older than Tori and her friends, but she knew a lot more about boys. Tori didn't like Veronica much, but she had to admit that Veronica was an expert in the dating department.

Jill could hear Tori shouting for Veronica and then a murmured conversation as Tori filled her in. A minute later, there was a click as Veronica picked up the phone extension in her room.

"Hello, Jill," Veronica said. "Need some romance advice?"

"Do I ever," Jill said. "I think Jesse really likes me, but he still hasn't asked me to the dance my school is having. I should just ask him, right?"

"Yeeek!" Veronica pretended to scream in horror. "Never, never, never! Jill, don't you know? The new thing is that you're supposed to pretend you don't even know Jesse exists. Play hard to get. Don't call him. Don't say hi first. Let him make all the moves."

"That makes no sense!" Jill said. "Jesse is one of my best friends. Why would I ignore him?"

"Because boys want to be the ones who do all that stuff," Veronica said. "They like the girl better if they think she's a prize they have to work hard for."

"That is the stupidest thing I ever heard," Haley piped up. "That makes it sound like the girl is just some trophy or something. Not a real person."

"Really," Jill agreed. She thought Veronica's advice sounded dumb—why would she act phony around Jesse all of a sudden? "Jesse and I respect each other. He likes it when I invite him to do stuff, like see a video. In fact, maybe I'll just ask *him* to the formal."

"All right, Jill!" Nikki cheered. "I bet he'd love it if you did. Maybe he just hasn't asked you because he feels shy."

"That's what Bronya said right before she left," Jill responded.

"Who's taking Bronya's place at the Academy?" Tori asked. Jill knew Tori had wanted to get into the Academy at one time. Then Tori had decided she didn't want to live away from home. Jill had been disappointed, but she respected Tori's decision. Still, Tori always wanted to hear what was going on at the Academy.

"Yeah. Can Tori take her place?" Veronica piped up. "The Academy is so nice and *far away* from here!"

"Be quiet, Veronica. I'm not going anywhere. If I left here, I'd probably come back and find you living in my room," Tori said. "Thanks for the boy advice—you can hang up now."

"Bye, Jill. Good luck with Jesse," Veronica said. There was a click.

"I have no idea who got picked," Jill went on. "All I know is that she's coming tonight or tomorrow. And that she'll never be as good a roommate as Bronya was."

"You don't know that, Jill," Haley said. "She might be really nice. In fact, I bet you anything she will be."

"I guess," Jill said glumly.

"What else is wrong?" Tori asked. "You sound kind of bummed."

"Nothing, except that I was late this morning and my coach chewed me out in front of the whole Academy," Jill answered. Her friends groaned in sympathy.

"That is so humiliating, isn't it?" Nikki said.

"Ludmila sounds even worse than Sarge." Sarge was the girls' nickname for Kathy Bart. She was the toughest coach at Silver Blades.

"Ludmila *is* worse," Jill said. "And with Sectionals in two weeks, she's even tougher than usual."

"Hey, Jill, too bad we're in different parts of the country. We don't get to go to Sectionals together," Tori said.

"Yeah, I know," Jill agreed. "Midwestern Sectionals are in Texas. Where are you guys going for Easterns?"

"Simsbury, Connecticut," Haley answered.

"Is anyone from Blade Runners going to be there?" Jill asked. The Blade Runners was a top skating club in Vermont. Its members always made a strong showing in their regional division. That meant the club usually sent at least one skater to the next-highest level of competition—Sectionals.

"Isn't someone from Blade Runners always there?" Tori said. "Someone who thinks she's the most beautiful, best skater in the world?"

"Meaning Carla Benson?" Jill teased. "Tori! You can't let Carla bother you. That will mess up your skating."

"It's Carla's fault," Tori wailed. "She always has to make everything into a personal contest!"

"Oh, come on, Tori, you can be pretty competitive, too," Haley pointed out.

"I can't help it," Tori responded. "I can't stand that smug look Carla gets on her perfect face when she places higher than I do!"

"Carla's not *that* bad. Just don't think about her," Jill advised. "Concentrate on your own skating."

"Are you on Carla's side?" Tori asked. "I can't believe it! Especially after what she did to you last summer at skating camp—that was so totally uncool. I mean, think about it, Jill. She made you look stupid in front of the boy you liked. She took you on a scary horseback ride. And she even admitted that she became friends with you because she thought it would help her get into the Academy."

"Are you still thinking about *that*? I'm not," Jill said. "I'm just saying that if you let Carla get to you, it's only going to hurt you, Tori."

"It won't hurt Carla, that's for sure," Haley said. "She never loses her concentration."

"Yeah, I guess you guys are right." Tori sighed. "It's just that Carla is so . . . so . . . *unlikable*."

"Which is why she's not even worth worrying about," Jill said. "Don't sink to her level."

"Okay, okay," Tori grumbled. "Anyway, we'd better go now. Veronica's probably in my room reading my diary or looking through my closet or something."

"It was great talking to you guys—you totally cheered me up after my rotten day," Jill said.

"Don't worry, Jill," Nikki said. "Ludmila will forgive you—just show up on time every day before Sectionals."

"Good luck with Jesse," Haley said. "Let us know what you decide to do about inviting him to the dance."

"Thanks. You guys are the best," Jill said. "Call me again soon, okay?"

The four girls said their good-byes, and Jill hung up the phone. She missed her friends back home so much. And now Bronya was gone, too. But my new roommate will be here soon, Jill reminded herself. Things will seem a lot less lonely after that.

Jill walked down the hall and pushed open the door of her room. She stared in amazement. There, in the middle of the floor, surrounded by a fancy set of white luggage, stood Carla Benson!

"Carla?" Jill said. "What are you doing here?"

"What do you *think* I'm doing here?" Carla said. "I'm your new roommate."

3

Jill realized that her mouth was hanging open. She shut it and tried to think of something to say.

"Well?" Carla said. "Aren't you going to congratulate me?"

"Um, congratulations," Jill said.

"Thanks." Carla smiled, showing off perfect, white teeth. "*Finally* Ludmila and Simon took me off that stupid waiting list. They've seen me skate a million times. I don't know why I didn't get accepted here sooner."

"Well, there are a lot of good people on that list," Jill said. "My friend Tori—"

Carla ignored Jill and kept talking. "Martin said there was nothing he could do about it, but I don't believe him. He just wasn't trying hard enough."

"Martin?" Jill repeated.

"Martin Fennell, my latest coach," Carla explained impatiently. "Haven't you ever heard of him?"

"Sure," Jill said. "But he's not the Blade Runners' coach, is he? He's in Chicago."

"You don't need to tell me he's in Chicago, Jill. I've been skating there for the past three months. Don't you ever read *Skating* magazine? It had an article about me switching over to Martin. And a picture."

"Oh," Jill said.

"Anyway, what they didn't put in the article is that Martin was on the British Olympic team with Simon Wells, like, a zillion years ago. That's the whole reason I switched to Martin."

Jill's eyes widened. "Because you thought he could get you moved up on the waiting list?"

"Duh! Of course." Carla flipped her long blond ponytail over her shoulder. "Isn't that what a coach is supposed to do? Help you?"

"Well, yes, but not like *that*," Jill said.

"Well, it didn't help anyway. I got in here because I'm a really good skater, in case you hadn't noticed," Carla said.

Carla looked around the room, a small frown on her face.

"Something's wrong here." Carla pointed to Jill's bed. Mr. Grizzly, the tattered stuffed bear Jill's younger sister Randi had given her, sat on her pillow. "What's your little . . . *baby toy* doing over there? That's supposed to be *my* bed."

Jill was flustered. "What do you mean?"

"That woman downstairs, Lisa What's-her-face, told me my bed was the one next to the window," Carla said.

"Oh, that was Bronya's bed—she was my roommate. But after she left, I took it," Jill said.

"But that side of the room is much better—anybody can see that," Carla objected. "You can't just *take* it."

"But I was here first," Jill pointed out.

Two red spots appeared on Carla's pale cheeks. "What are you saying? Do you think you're better than me just because you got into the Academy first?"

"No," Jill said. "I only meant—"

There was a knock on the door, and Lisa Welch stuck her head in. She was the dorm parent at Aspen House. She also coached some of the Academy's younger skaters.

"Oh, good, I see you girls have met. Everything going okay, Carla? Do you need anything?"

"Yes, as a matter of fact, I need my bed," Carla snapped.

Lisa looked confused. She glanced at the two beds. "Oh, Jill, did you move to Bronya's old bed?"

Jill nodded. "I hope that's okay. I didn't think it would matter if I switched sides, now that Bronya's gone."

"Well it *does* matter to *me*," Carla said. "So please just take all your stuff out of my side of the room."

"But I've been here longer," Jill protested. She

turned to Lisa. "Plus it took me a really long time to move it all over here!"

Lisa frowned. "Oh, girls, I hate to see you two starting off on the wrong foot like this. Jill, you probably should have spoken to me if you wanted to switch things around up here."

"I understand, Lisa," Jill answered in a low voice. "I just didn't think of it."

Carla raised her chin triumphantly.

"But now I think it makes sense to just leave things the way they are," Lisa said.

Carla's face fell. Jill smiled gratefully at Lisa.

"Carla, you'd better start unpacking all your things," Lisa advised. "You only have an hour until lights out, and you have a big first day tomorrow. Good night, girls." Lisa left the room.

Carla turned around and glared at Jill.

"Want me to help you unpack your stuff?" Jill offered meekly. She didn't want to fight with Carla or make Carla hate her.

"No, thank you," Carla said coldly.

She hurled one of her suitcases onto Jill's old bed and started yanking clothes out of it. Jill had never seen so many soft sweaters, faded jeans, and expensive leather shoes. Carla has even more clothes than Tori— and Tori has more clothes than anyone I know! Jill thought.

Carla strode over to Jill's new dresser and opened the top drawer.

"Um, Carla? That's my dresser," Jill said.

"What?" Carla stared at Jill. "You get the bigger dresser, too? I don't believe this!"

"But it goes with this side of the room," Jill said. "And it's only a tiny bit bigger."

"Fine," Carla snapped. She started putting her clothes into Jill's old dresser. Then she opened the closet.

"What's all this stuff?" Carla asked.

"It's mine," Jill said. "We have to share a closet. Everybody here does."

"This is ridiculous," Carla fumed. "My clothes alone won't fit in here." She pawed through Jill's skating dresses. "Half of these are made of Lycra," she said. "Why don't you just fold them and put them in a drawer? After all, you do have the bigger dresser."

"Sorry, Carla," Jill said, "but half the closet is mine."

"That is so selfish," Carla murmured.

Jill was stunned. She couldn't believe what a spoiled brat Carla was being. Jill decided not to say anything. She grabbed her school bag and lay on her bed. At least she could solve her math problems!

A few minutes later, Jill looked up from her homework. Carla was unpacking a trunk full of skating trophies, medals, and framed articles about herself. She started arranging them on the shelves above her bed.

Oh, brother, thought Jill. She tried not to laugh out loud. Just then, there was a knock on the door. Saved by the knock! Jill told herself.

"Come in," she called. Jesse popped his head into the room. Jill felt her heart skip a beat. She sat up quickly.

"Jesse, what are you doing here?" she asked. "It's almost lights out."

Jesse grinned. "What's the matter, aren't you glad to see me?" He walked in and then noticed Carla on the other side of the room. "Oh, hi. You must be Jill's new roommate."

Carla smiled and crossed the room. "Hi, I'm Carla. Who are you?"

"I'm Jesse. Hi, Carla." He turned to Jill. "I can only stay a minute. I promised Lisa I'd just run up and get my notebook."

"Notebook?" Jill repeated.

"Yeah, my red one," Jesse answered. He glanced around. "It must be here somewhere. I'm sure I had it with me yesterday when I came over."

Jill checked the cover of the notebook she was using for her math homework. It was red.

"Oops. Sorry, Jesse. I thought it was mine." She tore out her homework.

"Hey, Jill, not everything on the planet that's red is yours, you know," Jesse teased her.

Jill giggled. All her friends knew that red was Jill's absolute favorite color. She almost always wore red warm-ups to practice, and her bed was covered with a red afghan that her grandmother had crocheted.

Jill handed Jesse the notebook.

Carla cleared her throat loudly. "So, Jesse, how long have you been at the Academy?" she asked.

"A little over a year," Jesse answered, turning to her. "Before that, I trained at a rink in New Hampshire."

"New Hampshire, you're kidding!" Carla exclaimed. "I'm from Vermont!"

Jesse grinned. "Well, then, I guess we're practically neighbors."

"I used to be a member of the Blade Runners," Carla went on. "Maybe you've heard of them?"

"Yeah, I've heard of them. They're just about the best skating club in New England." Jesse sounded impressed.

"Thanks," Carla said sweetly. "So, neighbor, now that I'm here, maybe you can show me around the Academy."

"Okay, sure." Jesse shrugged. "Anyway, I better go before Lisa comes up here and yells at me for being in your room after lights out. Catch you both tomorrow."

"Nice meeting you, Jesse," Carla said.

"Same here," Jesse said, leaving the room.

"Bye!" Jill called. But Jesse was already gone.

"Whoa! What a cute guy!" Carla said, turning to Jill. "How long have you known *him*?"

"Since I got here, I guess," Jill answered. "But we've been really good friends for only a little while."

"*Friends?*" Carla's eyebrows went up. "You're not going out with him?"

"Well, no, not really," Jill admitted. But hopefully that will change soon, Jill added silently. She wasn't about to tell Carla how she felt.

Carla smiled and went back to her shelf of trophies. "Tell me more about Jesse. What does he skate?"

"Singles," Jill answered.

"Is he good?"

"Very," Jill answered. "He's one of the best male skaters here."

"Oh, really?" Carla arranged some medals. "So, where's he from in New Hampshire?"

Jill shrugged. "I don't remember. It's a small town."

Carla turned around again, a large trophy in her hand. "Does he have a girlfriend?"

Jill sighed in exasperation. "Why don't you ask him yourself, Carla?"

Carla raised her eyebrows and gave Jill a long look. "Maybe I will ask him," she finally said. "All I can say is that if he doesn't have a girlfriend, the girls at this Academy are all fools. *Big* fools."

Jill slammed her math book shut and grabbed her towel and toothbrush. She stalked down the hall to the bathroom. When she looked at herself in the mirror, she saw that she was still scowling.

Jill sighed. An hour ago, she'd been telling Tori not to let Carla get to her. Now it looked as if Jill would have to take her own advice—and it was going to be harder than she'd thought!

"Jill, is that really what you're wearing to practice today?" Carla asked.

It was six A.M. the next morning, and the two girls were getting dressed.

"Um, sure," Jill said, looking down at her faded sweatshirt and tattered red leggings. "Why?"

"It's kind of ratty-looking, is all. I guess some people don't mind looking sloppy when they skate," Carla said. "But I always like to look my best."

Jill sighed. "This outfit is fine, Carla."

Carla was pulling on an expensive-looking warm-up suit. The red and black pants and jacket fit her snugly. Jill had to admit that the suit looked great on the tall, slender girl.

"The kids in Blade Runners gave me this as a going-away present," Carla said. She stood in front of the mirror and smiled at herself.

Yeah, with a card that said DON'T COME BACK, Jill told herself. The thought made her giggle.

"What's so funny?" Carla said, scowling in Jill's direction. "What did the Silver Blades give you when you left?"

"Well, the Silver Blades colors are blue and silver. But they know I love red, so they gave me a red sweatshirt with the club logo." Jill began combing her hair.

"Just a sweatshirt?" Carla said. "Oh, too bad. I guess you weren't really good friends with the other members, huh?"

"It's a Silver Blades sweatshirt. And it meant a lot to me," Jill said, trying to keep her tone patient. "And the other members are good friends of mine. Some of them are my best friends."

Carla pointed to the little gold crown embroidered on her jacket. "This warm-up suit is a Royale. They make the absolute *best* warm-ups."

"It doesn't have to be a contest," Jill mumbled, yanking the comb through her hair.

"What's that?" asked Carla.

"Nothing," Jill said. "Come on, Carla. We'd better get to the dining hall for breakfast or we'll miss all the good food."

"And this is the arena," Jill said. It's also the last thing I promised to show you this morning, she added to herself.

Carla looked around, studying everything carefully. The arena's lobby had a row of large windows facing the Rocky Mountains. Comfortable couches and chairs were set up around a wood-burning stove. A glass wall looked onto the rink, which was surrounded by huge potted trees. The ceiling had skylights that let natural light fall on the ice.

"It's nice enough, I guess," Carla said after a long pause.

Jill rolled her eyes. She waved her arm toward a corridor lined with doors. "Those doors are to the weight rooms and the exercise studios. There's even a whirlpool room for hydrotherapy," she said. "The changing rooms are over there. And here's the bulletin board where they hang notices about rink times and stuff like that. You should check it every week."

As Jill glanced at the board, a pink flyer caught her eye.

JOIN THE ICE PALS PROGRAM!
HELP BRIGHTEN A CHILD'S DAY.
ICE PALS PAIRS SICK CHILDREN WITH
YOUNG SKATERS AS PEN PALS.
BE THE STUDENT COORDINATOR AT YOUR
SKATING SCHOOL OR RINK!
SEE YOUR COACH FOR DETAILS.

"Wow! What a great idea," Jill said when she had finished reading.

"You think?" said Carla, who'd been reading over her shoulder. "It seems kind of babyish. Why would you want to be someone's pen pal?"

"It's for sick little kids who want to get letters from skaters," Jill said. "That's why."

"But how does that help my skating?" Carla asked in a bored voice.

"It doesn't, Carla," Jill said, shaking her head in disbelief. "It helps someone else."

"Whatever," Carla said. "Let's put our skates on."

The girls walked into the rink a few minutes later. Ludmila strode over to them. "Good morning, girls. Welcome, Carla."

Carla smiled eagerly. "Thank you, Ludmila. I'm so excited to be here. I can't wait to get out on the ice."

"Make sure you warm up well first," Ludmila advised.

"I will," Carla assured her. "But I'm very limber. Are we going to work together after I warm up, Ludmila? I'd really like to get some help from you on my triple toe loop. I want it to be perfect for Sectionals." Carla smiled sweetly.

"I'm happy to see that you are so eager, Carla," Ludmila said. "Why don't you work on your own after you warm up? I'll come to you in a while."

Jill saw Carla frown when Ludmila turned away from her.

"Jill, I want to go over your routine with you first

thing," Ludmila said. "Let me know when you have warmed up, and we will get started."

Ludmila walked off, and Carla scowled. "I don't see why she has to work with *you* first. That isn't fair. I'm new here."

"Ludmila works with different skaters at different times. She doesn't explain why, but I'm sure she has her reasons," Jill said.

Carla tossed her hair. "Maybe Ludmila figures I don't need much coaching."

"Every skater needs coaching, Carla," Jill pointed out. She sat on the floor and stretched her inner thigh muscles in a straddle position.

Carla shrugged and smiled thinly. "Some skaters need more help than others." She sat down near Jill and copied her position. "You know what's a really good stretch? To go from this straight into a split. That is, if you can do a split." Carla slid easily from her straddle into a full split on the floor.

"Of course I can do a split," Jill responded, sliding into one.

"Good try. Too bad your back knee is bent a little bit," Carla said.

Jill straightened her back knee. "There. No problem."

"I usually do this now." Carla leaned forward and grasped her ankle. "It's really good for stretching out your lower back and your hamstrings. You'd better not try it, though. It's an advanced move."

Jill matched Carla's position. "No problem for me. Doesn't hurt a bit."

Carla narrowed her eyes at Jill. "Here's the tough part. I was the only person at Blade Runners who could do this." With her body still flat against her front leg, Carla reached back with one hand. She bent her back leg and grabbed her ankle. Then she pulled her calf toward her thigh. "Mmm, that feels so good. It's great for your quadriceps—those are your thigh muscles."

"I know what a quadricep is," Jill snapped. She reached back and grabbed her ankle. As she began to pull it toward her, she felt a twinge of pain in her thigh.

"Don't pull it as far as I am," Carla said. "Your body isn't used to this."

"Oh, I'm used to it. I do this all the time," Jill replied. She pulled her ankle harder. Her thigh was burning, but she struggled not to wince.

"Be careful, Jill!" Carla said sweetly. "You have to learn your body's limits. Some people just aren't naturally limber."

Jill scowled and gave her ankle one last yank. As she did, she felt a searing pain in her thigh. She let out a scream.

"What's wrong? What happened?" Carla cried.

Several skaters hurried over. Jill released her leg and pulled it in front of her. She frantically rubbed her throbbing thigh muscle.

"Jill, are you okay?" Sarah Miller asked.

"What happened?" Francie Morrell asked, kneeling next to Jill.

Jill could hear Ludmila's voice from the back of the crowd. "Let me through. Get out of the way, please." Ludmila appeared at Jill's side. "Jill, what is it? Are you hurt?"

Carla knelt down by Jill and Ludmila. "I think it's my fault, Ludmila. I was warming up, just doing my usual routine. Jill was trying to copy me. She must have pushed her stretch too far."

Ludmila looked stern. "Jill, your warm-up is serious business. It is not a contest." She carefully felt Jill's thigh. "Let's hope this is a minor muscle pull. Dr. Perlberg is working with a student in the whirlpool room. We'll have her check you out."

"I'll help you walk to the doctor, Jill," Carla piped up. "I sure hope you're okay. You wouldn't want to miss Sectionals because of an injury."

Jill glared at her. "Something tells me you'd like that a lot, Carla!"

Ludmila frowned. "Jill, I'm very surprised at you! Carla is trying to help."

"Really, Jill. I'm just trying to help," Carla said.

Jill gritted her teeth. She couldn't believe what a complete fake Carla was. And she couldn't believe she'd been stupid enough to sink to Carla's level, competing with her over a stupid warm-up exercise!

Jill suddenly knew exactly what Tori had meant on the phone the night before. Carla *did* turn everything into a contest. Now Carla was competing with Jill. And so far, Jill was losing!

5

"No skating today or tomorrow!" Dr. Perlberg's voice rang in Jill's ears. She had checked Jill's leg. Jill had a pulled muscle. "Ice it today. No skating this afternoon or tomorrow," the doctor had said.

"But Sectionals—" she'd started to say.

"No buts!" Dr. Perlberg had said. "Sectionals is one competition. You need these legs to last your whole life."

That was easy for her to say, Jill thought as she headed back toward the rink. But Sectionals winners went on to Nationals. And the winners at Nationals would represent the United States at World and Olympic events. Right now, getting ready for Sectionals *was* Jill's whole life!

When she got back to the rink, she saw Ludmila

working with Carla. Jill leaned against the boards and watched.

Carla skated in wide, graceful circles. She turned and began a series of powerful backward crossovers. Then she leaped easily into a triple Lutz, followed by a double toe loop. She landed solidly and continued around the rink.

Carla's skating was smooth and athletic. And she wasn't even breathing hard, Jill realized.

"Okay, Carla—let's see that triple toe loop," Ludmila called from the center of the ice. A few other skaters stopped to watch.

Carla glided down the rink and then launched herself into the jump. She had good momentum and great height, easily making three rotations before landing smoothly with her arms outstretched and her chin raised. Her form had been flawless, as far as Jill could see. That was the jump Carla wanted to work on? Jill thought.

Alice David, who was only eight and the youngest skater at the Academy, stood near Jill. "Wow. Did you see that? Who is she?"

"My new roommate," Jill said miserably.

"Nice work, Carla!" Ludmila shouted.

Carla grinned. Then she glanced over and saw Jill watching. Her grin grew even wider. Jill had seen Carla skate before. She had always been good. But now she was incredible. Carla would clearly be one of the strongest competitors at Sectionals.

"Come over, please," Ludmila called. Carla skated

to the middle of the rink. Jill watched as they talked. Ludmila used hand gestures and moved her feet every now and then to demonstrate something. Then Ludmila patted Carla's arm and started walking toward the gate. Carla skated along next to her.

"Ah, Jill," Ludmila said. "You're back. What did the doctor say?"

Jill quickly explained Dr. Perlberg's advice. Ludmila nodded as she listened.

"I'm glad it's not serious," Ludmila said. "But you'll have to work extra hard to make up the lost time, Jill. Not to mention the fifteen minutes you lost yesterday morning when you decided to stay in your nice warm bed."

Jill flinched. Then she saw that Ludmila was smiling. Behind her, Carla's eyes had narrowed, and she was grinning in an unfriendly way.

"I'll make up the time, Ludmila," Jill promised, trying to ignore Carla. "Can I talk to you about something else? It's about that sign on the bulletin board. The one about the Ice Pals program?"

"Oh, yes," Ludmila responded. "That's a wonderful organization. They're doing some important work for sick children."

"I'd really like to help out. The sign said they're looking for volunteers from each skating school," Jill said.

Ludmila raised her eyebrows. "You'd like to be the Ice Pals coordinator for the Academy? Well, that's a lovely thought, Jill, but it's a lot of responsibility. It

means finding kids here who are willing to participate, pairing them with children from the Ice Pals list,
and then keeping track of everything."

"I think I'd like doing it," Jill assured her.

"But that's not all," Ludmila went on. "As a coordinator, you'd also be expected to appear in the Ice Pals
exhibition."

Carla perked up. "An exhibition?" she asked. "Is it
going to be on TV?"

"I've seen it on cable in the past," Ludmila said.
"The exhibition raises money for the Ice Pals project.
Student coordinators from all over the country perform. But Jill, the show is only two days before Sectionals. I'm concerned that it might be too much for
you right now."

"I really think I can handle this *and* Sectionals,
Ludmila," Jill said. "Organizing the letter writing
won't be too hard. And I could perform the routine
I'm doing for Sectionals in the show."

"What a great idea!" Carla said with enthusiasm. "I
can perform *my* routine at the show, too!" She
stopped and lowered her voice. "I mean, I'd really like
to be an Ice Pals coordinator, too, Ludmila."

Jill stared at her. "But when we saw the poster earlier, you said—"

Carla cut her off. "When I saw the poster I didn't
know how important the program is for all those little
kids."

Jill couldn't believe her ears. "Carla, that's not
true—" she began. Then she stopped. The last thing

Jill wanted was for Ludmila to see her yelling at Carla again.

Ludmila glanced from Jill to Carla and back to Jill. "You know, I think it might be a very good idea for the two of you to work on this together," she said finally. "As long as you don't let it interfere with your skating, of course. I'll tell the Ice Pals committee that the Academy has *two* volunteer coordinators."

Jill couldn't believe her ears! It was bad enough to be stuck rooming with Carla—but now she had to work with her on Ice Pals, too? Then Jill laughed to herself. She had a funny feeling she wouldn't be working with Carla on Ice Pals, because Carla wouldn't do any of the work. But Jill was sure about one thing—Carla *would* take all the credit!

"Jesse!" Jill cried eagerly. She picked up her tray from the lunch line and walked across the dining hall. She and Jesse had different classes, so they tried to eat together as often as they could. She couldn't wait to tell him about how awful Carla was and about her pulled muscle.

As she got closer to his table, she saw that Jesse wasn't alone. Carla was sitting across from him, chatting nonstop and smiling widely.

Jill's heart sank. She had been looking forward to eating with Jesse alone. She had even thought that today she might get up the courage to ask Jesse to the formal.

Silently, Jill slid into the seat beside Jesse.

He looked at her. "Hi, Jill!" he said.

"Hi, Jesse." Jill smiled. "Hi, Carla," she added politely.

"Carla was just telling me about this incredible project she's working on," Jesse explained. "Actually, Jill, it sounds like something you might be interested in. Carla, tell Jill about your pen-pals project."

Jill almost choked on the bite of pasta salad she'd just taken. "*Your* pen-pals project, Carla?"

"Well, it's not *my* project," Carla responded. "It's an Ice Pals project. But I'm so excited about it that I feel like it's my project." Carla looked at Jesse and sighed deeply. "I'd do just about anything to help somebody."

"I'm sure it doesn't hurt that you get to be in an ice show on cable TV, either," Jill commented.

Jesse turned to Jill and frowned. "What are you talking about, Jill?"

"Didn't Carla tell you?" Jill asked. "All the Ice Pals coordinators are going to be in an ice show in Kansas City. It's probably going to be on cable TV."

"Oh, that." Carla waved her hand. "I forgot about the show. I just want to help sick kids."

Jesse smiled. "That's fantastic, Carla."

"You know, I volunteered to be an Ice Pals coordinator, too," Jill put in.

"That's great, Jill," Jesse said. "I'm sure Carla can use lots of help with it."

"I volunteered *before* Carla," Jill said. Then she winced. That had sounded so babyish. It made *her* look bad, not Carla.

Carla leaned across the table and put one of her hands over Jesse's. "Can I count on you to be a pen pal for one of these kids?"

"Sure thing, Carla. You got it." Jesse's voice was earnest.

Jill's mouth dropped open. *She* had planned on asking Jesse to volunteer. And now Carla was acting as if she were Mother Teresa on skates.

There was a clanging sound as Kevin Olsen, another Academy skater, stood up on a chair and hit his spoon against his glass. The room quieted down.

"Announcement! Announcement!" Kevin boomed. "Anyone who wants to work on the decorating committee for the formal, come and talk to me before lunch is over!"

Kevin sat back down, and the chatter in the room grew loud again.

Carla leaned across the table toward Jesse, her green eyes flashing. "The formal, what's that?" she asked eagerly.

"This big dance they have here every year," Jesse responded.

"It sounds exciting," Carla said. "Is it really formal? I mean, does everybody get dressed up?"

Jesse nodded. "It's the biggest Academy event of the year. They hire a band and everything."

"Wow, a band!" Carla exclaimed. "I love dancing to live music. Don't you?"

"Me too," Jill put in quickly. "Live music is the best."

Carla ignored her. "Where do they have the formal, Jesse?"

"Actually, I think it's in here," Jesse said. "But Kevin told me they decorate so it looks really good." He shrugged. "I didn't go last year, though, so I'm not sure."

"Why didn't you go?" Jill and Carla asked at the same time. Carla shot Jill an annoyed look and then focused back on Jesse.

Jesse's face reddened. "Well, I was new here. I didn't know anyone. It was stupid, I guess. I should have just gone alone."

"I know how you feel, Jesse," Carla said softly. "I wouldn't have gone alone either."

Jesse gave Carla a sympathetic smile. "But that's what I'm saying. I *should* have gone alone. I guess I just felt too shy or something."

"I understand perfectly," Carla said. She ran her hand through her long hair. "I'm really shy, too."

Carla's about as shy as a game-show host! Jill thought, squirming uncomfortably in her seat. She couldn't stand watching Carla flirt with Jesse for another second! Jill cleared her throat loudly. "I guess lunch is over. We all better get going right away or we'll be late for classes," she announced.

Jesse looked up in surprise. "Is it time already?" He checked his watch.

"I'll catch up with you guys in a moment," Carla said. "I just want to stop and talk to that guy about joining the decorations committee for the formal."

Jill was surprised. "Are you kidding, Carla?"

"Why not?" Carla said. "It sounds like fun! Besides, I love deciding how things should look. Especially for dances and stuff. I'm really good at it, too."

"But you already volunteered to be an Ice Pals coordinator," Jill pointed out.

"Oh." Carla looked disappointed. Then her face brightened. "Well, I'm sure I'll still have time for the decorating committee. See you later. Bye, Jesse!"

"Bye!" Jesse called after her.

Jill turned to him and shook her head. "Can you believe her?"

"I know," Jesse responded. "She's amazing. I guess it's like she said, she really *does* like to help people."

Jill stared at Jesse. She couldn't believe he had fallen for Carla's act.

"Somehow I don't think Carla's trying to help other people," Jill finally said.

Jesse turned to face her. "What are you talking about, Jill?"

"If you ask me, the only person Carla's interested in helping is *herself*," Jill snapped.

"Why would you say something like that?" Jesse asked. "Carla seems really sweet, wanting to help those sick kids and everything. And it's nice that she wants to join the decorating committee. She doesn't know anyone here. It'll be a great way for her to meet some people. Right now, you and I are her only friends."

Jill didn't know what to say. She didn't consider herself Carla's friend—not after the way Carla had been acting. But Jill didn't want Jesse to think she was unfriendly.

"It's just that I don't know how serious Carla can be about her skating if she's going to waste time decorating the dining hall," Jill blurted out. She instantly regretted saying it. A lot of kids at the Academy managed to fit things in between eating, breathing, and sleeping skating. She wouldn't have minded being on the decorating committee herself if she hadn't already volunteered for Ice Pals.

"The decorating committee is not a waste of time," Jesse said, standing up. "And we're going to make it look fantastic in here."

"You mean—" Jill started to say.

"I mean, I'm already on the decorating committee," Jesse said. "I'll see you later, Jill."

He picked up his tray and walked off.

6

"Wha . . . ?" Carla mumbled in her sleep. Then she snored and rolled over.

Across the room, Jill sighed and pulled her pillow over her head. Carla had talked, muttered, and snored all night long. Every time Jill had managed to doze off, Carla's talking had wakened her again. If only the people who saw her do a perfect triple toe loop could see her now, Jill thought.

Finally, the first ray of morning light shined through the window. Jill slipped out of bed and wrapped herself in her thick red bathrobe.

She crept down the stairs and across the common room. Then she rapped on the door of Lisa Welch's apartment.

A moment later, Lisa came to the door. She was still in her plaid flannel pajamas.

"Jill," Lisa said, yawning. "You're up early. What can I do for you?"

"Sorry to bother you, Lisa," Jill said. "But it's about Carla being my new roommate. I was just wondering . . ."

"Yes?" said Lisa.

"I don't know how to put this without sounding like a baby," Jill said. "But I just don't like her. I was wondering if there was any way she could switch rooms with someone else."

Lisa frowned. "You'd better come in, Jill."

Minutes later, Jill was sitting on Lisa's couch sipping a cup of hot tea.

"So what's the problem?" Lisa asked.

Jill quickly explained what Carla had done to her at skating camp the summer before. Then she told Lisa about Carla's behavior since she'd arrived at the Academy. Lisa listened in silence, sipping her own tea every now and then. Then she put her cup down.

"Jill, I can see that you and Carla have your difficulties. And that you feel a little threatened by her now. But you're going to meet a lot of people in life you don't like. And you're going to have to learn how to deal with them."

Jill picked at the hem of her bathrobe.

"I guess I could try," she finally said.

"That's the spirit," Lisa said. "Is it possible that you've misunderstood some of Carla's actions—or some of the things she's said?"

"No, Lisa. I really don't think so," Jill answered.

"Let's look at this logically. You think she wanted to be in Ice Pals only because she heard there was a show. That's not exactly nice. But even if it's true, is there anything truly terrible about a skater's wanting to be on TV?" Lisa asked.

"I guess not," Jill mumbled.

"You also said she volunteered to be on the decorating committee for the formal. And the boy you like, Jesse, is on the committee. But did Carla know that before she volunteered?"

"I don't think so." Jill shook her head miserably. She could see where this was leading. Somehow, even when Carla wasn't around, she still managed to make Jill look bad!

"Do you think it's possible that Carla's feeling a little lonely and a little homesick? And that's why she volunteered for Ice Pals and the decorating committee—even if it might be more than she can handle?"

"I guess so," Jill said.

"Jill, Carla needs a friend here. And it would be great if you could become that friend," Lisa said. "But, if not, you still need to find a way to get along with her. There aren't any open spots in the dorm. And I don't think it would be fair to ask someone else to switch rooms. Do you?"

"No. I guess not," said Jill, standing up. "Thanks anyway, Lisa."

"No problem, Jill. Keep me posted," Lisa said. "I'm

here for all the girls in Aspen House. If you still have a problem, come talk to me again. I'll see what I can do."

Jill walked back up the stairs with her shoulders slumped. As she passed the pay phone at the end of the hall, she suddenly missed Tori. Tori would know exactly what to do about Carla. And she'd know Jill wasn't exaggerating!

Jill tiptoed into her room and opened her top desk drawer. She fished around for the phone calling card her parents had given her to use in emergencies. This is an emergency, Jill reasoned. She was stuck with the worst roommate in the world. And now Jesse was mad at her!

Jill breathed a sigh of relief when Tori answered the phone. "Hi, Tori, it's me," Jill said. "Sorry I'm calling so early."

"Jill? Hi!" Tori sounded sleepy. "Are you okay?"

"Oh, Tori, I didn't know who else to call. You're never going to believe who my new roommate is," Jill said. "Carla Benson."

"Carla Benson?" Tori shrieked. "I can't believe she got into the Academy. She was stuck-up before! Now she'll be totally impossible!"

"She's been really mean to me," Jill agreed. "She's constantly trying to get me to compete with her."

"You mean about skating?" Tori asked.

"About everything!" Jill cried. "Warm-up exercises, practice clothes, which side of the room she wants—and now she's after Jesse!"

"Oh, Jill, I don't think you have to worry about Jesse," Tori assured her. "From what you've told me, he's a really nice guy. I'm sure he'd never fall for someone like Carla."

"But that's the problem. Carla's not *like* Carla when he's around. She puts on this whole fake sweet act," Jill said. "And I think Jesse's mad at me right now. I'm worried. What if he starts to like Carla better than me?"

"He never would," Tori said. "But why is he mad at you?"

"Because I made some stupid comment about how the decorating committee was a waste of time. It turns out he's on the decorating committee," Jill said.

"Ouch. That's pretty bad," Tori said. "After we all spoke the other day, Veronica showed me a magazine article. It was all about what she told you—how girls are supposed to play hard to get and everything."

"What are you talking about?" Jill asked.

"Well, the article also says you aren't supposed to say negative things. You're supposed to be upbeat and positive when you're around the boy you like."

"Carla must have memorized that article," Jill said sourly.

"Then maybe you should, too," Tori said. "Hang on. I'm going to get Veronica. I'll tell her to bring the magazine."

A minute later, Veronica came on.

"Jill?" Veronica said. "Sit down. And get ready to take notes."

"Jill, wait up!"

Jesse jogged up to Jill outside the dining hall later that day. "Hey," he panted. "I've been following you for the last five minutes. Didn't you hear me shouting?"

"Oh, hi, Jesse." Jill kept walking. Act like you're not interested, she told herself. "I'm rushing to English class. I don't want to be late."

"Well, where were you yesterday afternoon and this morning? I didn't see you in practice," Jesse said.

"Didn't Carla tell you?" Jill asked. "I pulled a thigh muscle. I'm fine, though. I'll be back on the ice tomorrow."

"Jill! Will you stop walking for a minute and talk to me?" Jesse said. He held Jill's arm gently. "You pulled a muscle? Why didn't you say something at lunch yesterday afternoon?" he asked. He looked hurt.

Because you were too busy flirting with Carla and then you were mad at me for saying that stupid thing about the decorating committee! Jill wanted to shout. She remembered the magazine article Veronica had read to her over the phone and gritted her teeth.

"Oh, it just slipped my mind, I guess! I'm *fine*, though, really," Jill said. "I've got to go, Jesse. See you!"

Jill pushed through the dining-hall door. When she glanced back, she saw Jesse standing there, staring after her. She forced herself to head for the stairs to the classrooms.

Jill couldn't believe what had just happened. Jesse hadn't been mad at her—he'd been worried!

She had acted as if everything were fine and as if she were in a rush to get to class. Then Jesse had looked at her as if his heart were about to break.

The magazine article was right! Jill thought. Playing hard to get works! Well, if that was all it took, Jesse will be asking me to the dance in no time!

7

Jill took a deep breath and launched into her routine's final jumps, a triple flip and double toe loop. She landed solidly, then did some back crossovers. Finally she wound down into a fast, tight sit spin, then rose to a standing spin, with her arms lifted over her head.

Yes, she thought triumphantly as the last notes of her music faded. She had nailed her routine. It felt great to be back on the ice, doing what she loved best.

"Good work, Jill!" Ludmila called. "That pulled thigh muscle isn't bothering you too much?"

It had been several days since she hurt her leg. The first few times she skated, it had ached a little. But now it was fine.

"It doesn't hurt a bit," Jill said, grinning at Ludmila.

She looked toward the end of the rink and saw that Carla was skating in small circles and watching her.

"All right, work on your own," Ludmila instructed. She waved to Carla on the other side of the ice. "Let's get to work, Carla," she shouted. "We'll try it with music today."

Jill skated to a corner of the rink and hiked up her leggings. She smoothed back her ponytail and took a deep breath. She started to position herself for the opening of her routine, with her head turned over her right shoulder. Then she spotted Carla across the ice, pushing off for her triple toe loop. Carla's form was flawless, as usual.

Suddenly Jill heard Carla's words from the other day echo in her head: "Maybe Ludmila figures I don't need much coaching." Carla certainly didn't need help with her triple toe loop.

Jill glanced back across the ice in time to see Carla perform a tuck axel followed by another perfect triple toe loop. Carla sailed over the ice, her face shining with happiness and her eyes scanning the rink to see who was watching her.

Jill took a deep breath and tried to shake off her thoughts. Don't worry about how Carla is skating, she reminded herself. Just concentrate on performing your own personal best.

Taking her position again, Jill launched into the back crossovers that started her routine. The first jump in her routine, a double axel, was an easy one for Jill. As she sailed through it, her confidence returned.

She was almost done with her routine when she heard a shout.

"Watch it!" Carla yelled, skidding to a stop. She had almost collided with Jill.

"Wow, sorry, Carla!" Jill said. She knew it had been her fault. Skaters working on their own were supposed to watch out for skaters being coached.

"I'm sure you're sorry," Carla hissed. "You'd just love it if you messed me up, wouldn't you?"

"No, Carla! It's not like that," Jill said. "Honestly!"

"Sure it's not," Carla whispered, glancing back to see if Ludmila could hear her. "Was it an accident when you told your friend over the phone the other morning that you're stuck with me as a roommate? I heard you when I was walking to the bathroom."

"Carla—" Jill started to say.

"You just do whatever you feel like doing, don't you, Jill? Like taking my side of the room," Carla said. "Well, maybe I'll start doing whatever I feel like doing!" She narrowed her eyes at Jill and then spun around and skated off. "Just an accident!" she called cheerfully to Ludmila.

Jill stood there, gaping at Carla. She couldn't believe what she'd just heard. Carla was the one who does whatever she wants, Jill told herself. And it seems like all she ever wants to do is be mean to me!

Fine, Jill thought. If Carla wants to turn everything into a contest, I'll play along. And I'll make sure I do everything better!

"Hi, Francie. Hi, Sarah. Mind if I join you?" Jill pulled a chair up to a table in the Academy's library that night. The small library was above the dining hall, near the classrooms.

Jill didn't feel like going back to her room and seeing Carla until the last possible minute. The library was a perfect place to hide out. Carla doesn't seem like the kind of person who would spend a lot of time here, Jill thought.

"Hi, Jill. How's it going?" Sarah asked.

"Hi, Jill," Francie echoed. "Let me make some room for you." She pushed aside a pile of open books and papers.

"Have you guys written your letters to your Ice Pals yet?" Jill asked, pulling her English book from her school bag.

"No," Francie said. She and Sarah exchanged puzzled looks.

"But you are going to be in Ice Pals, right?" Jill asked.

"Well . . . ," Sarah said. Her voice trailed off.

"Um, I'm not sure," Francie added.

"Is it because you're worried that it'll take too much

time away from your skating?" Jill asked. She couldn't understand why anyone wouldn't want to participate. It didn't take that much time to write a couple of letters every month.

There was a long pause at the table. Finally Jill understood what was going on.

"You guys have never heard of Ice Pals, have you?" she asked.

"No," said Francie. "But I was embarrassed to admit it because it sounded like some important skating thing we were supposed to know about."

"Me neither," Sarah said. "What is it?"

Jill quickly explained, telling them about the letter she had already written to her Ice Pal, an eight-year-old girl named Kim.

"Wow, it sounds awesome. Count me in," Sarah said.

"Me too!" Francie added. "Can I write to a little girl, too?"

"I want a boy," said Sarah. "I have three little sisters at home, and I always wanted a brother."

"No problem," Jill said. "I have the list of kids that Ludmila gave me right here."

The three girls bent their heads over the list. A minute later, Sarah and Francie had jotted down the names and addresses of their new pen pals.

"Hey, Jill, why did you think we already knew all about Ice Pals?" Sarah asked.

"Carla and I are both coordinators," said Jill. "We split the names of all the Academy students into two lists. We were both supposed to talk to the people on our lists by today." Except it looks like only one of us did, Jill added silently.

"And we were on Carla's list?" Francie said. "Because I talked to Carla in the locker room this afternoon and she didn't mention Ice Pals once."

"We have the same English tutor, and she didn't say anything to me, either," Sarah added. "All she could talk about was Sectionals and how she was going to win. She even wanted to write her essay on it!"

"Carla has a one-track mind. All she talked about in the locker room was how she couldn't wait to beat a certain someone at Sectionals," Francie said.

" 'A certain someone'? She really said that?" Sarah giggled.

Jill didn't think it was very funny. She had a feeling that "certain someone" was her! Jill gathered her schoolbooks and stuffed them back into her canvas bag. Then she stood up and yanked on her parka.

"Well, I have to get going, you guys. Thanks for being in Ice Pals," Jill said. "See you tomorrow."

"See you tomorrow, Jill," both girls said.

Jill ran down the stairs and into the cold night air. She was so angry she could hardly think straight. Carla hadn't even spoken to the Academy students on her half of the list. It was bad enough that she had joined the program only to be in the skating show. But what about all those sick kids who'd wait for a letter and never get one? Jill had six little brothers and sisters at home—she knew that, for a little kid, even a week or two could seem like forever. Especially for a sick kid stuck in a hospital bed.

Carla is a complete and total selfish jerk! Jill thought. As she raced back to the dorm, she grew angrier and angrier. She couldn't wait to get to her room and tell Carla exactly what she thought of her.

Jill stomped across the porch of Aspen House and flung open the front door, letting it slam behind her. She stormed across the common room. Alice David was sitting on the couch in front of the television. Her eyes lit up when she saw Jill.

"Jill!" she cried. "I'm watching a video. Want to watch with me?"

"Later, Alice," Jill muttered, storming by. She took the stairs two at a time and flew down the hall. The door of her room was closed and there was a note on it.

Jill,

I'm at a decorating committee meeting and I'll be back late. I guess I'll need a big, strong boy to walk me home—lucky for me that Jesse is on the committee too! Anyway, even if my desk light bothers you, please keep it on because I don't want to fumble around in the dark when I get back. Hope you like what I did to the room!

Carla

"Like what you did to the room?" Jill mumbled. She threw the door open. And blinked in the dim light from her desk lamp. Why was her desk light on? And why did her bed look different? Where was her red afghan and Mr. Grizzly, the stuffed bear? Where was the framed picture of her parents that usually sat on her bedside table?

Then Jill realized what had happened.

Jill's things were back where they'd been before Bronya left. Carla had switched all her things to Jill's side of the room!

8

"**H**i, Jill, did you like . . ." Carla stopped talking. Her eyes grew wide as she took in the room.

While Carla had been at her meeting, Jill had switched everything back. It had taken her almost two hours, and she was dead tired. But the look of shock on Carla's face made it all worthwhile.

"Oh, hi, Carla!" Jill said. She put down the book she was reading. "You can cross Francie and Sarah off your list of students to talk to about Ice Pals. I signed them up."

"That's nice," Carla said, still glancing around the room. "I guess you didn't like what I did in here," she finally said.

"Not really. So I switched stuff back. I hope that's okay," Jill said, struggling not to laugh. "Have you written to your own Ice Pal, by the way?"

Carla shrugged. "Oh, you mean Timmy?"

"Tommy," Jill corrected. "Your Ice Pal is Tommy Schuman."

"Timmy, Tommy. Anyway, I'll write to him soon," Carla replied. "I'm just really busy right now. There's Sectionals, and there's all the work I'm doing for the decorating committee." She hung up her jacket and started changing into her pajamas.

"How *was* the decorating-committee meeting?" Jill asked.

"Great! I'm the president now, you know. It's really a lot of responsibility. Plus, I've been seeing Jesse after every meeting."

Jill's eyes widened. "S-Seeing Jesse?" she stammered. "What are you talking about?"

"Oh, didn't you know?" Carla flashed Jill a smile. She sat down at her desk and pulled out her hairbrush. "Jesse and I have gotten really close lately. We're both on the committee, and I've been helping him with his math homework after every meeting. Math is one of my best subjects." She giggled. "And believe me, Jesse needs a *lot* of help."

Jill's stomach tightened. "He didn't say anything to *me* about having trouble in math."

Carla began running the brush through her long blond hair. "One hundred strokes every night," she sang. "Actually, Jesse and I didn't talk much about math tonight. The meeting ran long because the committee can't decide whether the formal's theme should be 'The Four Seasons' or 'Dancing in the Moonlight.' "

She giggled again. "Of course, Jesse liked 'Dancing in the Moonlight.' It's so much more romantic, don't you think?"

Jill felt sick. "Romantic?" she repeated.

"Sure," Carla responded. "Can't you just picture it? The ceiling of the dining hall will be covered with silver stars, and the whole room will be filled with twinkling blue lights." She let out a sigh. "Perfect for slow dancing."

"Yeah, perfect," Jill agreed miserably. But who would Jesse be slow dancing *with*—Jill or Carla?

Jill woke with a start. Something was wrong! The room was way too bright for early morning. She glanced at her alarm clock. Eight A.M.! Her stomach lurched. She had overslept by two hours!

Jill threw off her covers and jumped up. Carla's bed was empty, and her skate bag was gone. As Jill rushed around the room, throwing on clothes and grabbing her school things, she tried to figure out why her new alarm clock hadn't worked.

She pictured herself switching her stuff with Carla's the night before. She *knew* she had moved her clock and reset the alarm. She knew because it had been flashing 12:00. She'd double-checked the instructions before she reset the clock and turned the alarm on.

Jill stopped and looked at the black, plastic clock.

The alarm button was set to OFF. And on top of the button was a thick, greasy smudge. Jill wiped her finger over the smudge. It felt like hand cream. She held her hand under her nose and smelled a sharp orange scent—that was the scent of the cream Carla used every day!

Jill raced downstairs and over to the arena. When she dashed inside to the rink, she saw Ludmila working with Sarah Miller. Ludmila glanced up and saw Jill standing next to the boards.

"Work on your own for a minute," she told Sarah. Ludmila walked over to Jill slowly. At the far end of the rink, Carla saw what was happening. She skated closer and pretended to be practicing her footwork nearby.

Ludmila stood in front of Jill for a minute, then looked down at her watch and back at Jill.

"So," she finally said quietly. "You have decided to grace us with your presence today?"

Jill gripped her hands together so Ludmila wouldn't see that they were shaking. "I know you won't believe this," Jill said. "But I set my new alarm clock last night and it didn't go off this morning."

Carla skated a little closer. Then she smiled. Jill felt like jumping over the boards and shaking her.

"You are wrong, Jill. I do believe you," Ludmila said. "The problem is, I do not accept this excuse. We have already talked about this. The problem with excuses is that they don't improve your skating. I would rather have you set five alarm clocks than make one more excuse."

"I understand," Jill said quietly. "But—"

"But! But! But!" Ludmila said, cutting Jill off. "Jill, starting today you are on probation for a month. If you are late for practice during the next month—even once—we are going to sit down and have a long conference call with your parents."

Jill couldn't believe it. She glanced away from Ludmila and saw that Carla was still skating nearby. But Carla wasn't smiling anymore. She looked pale and frightened. Good! Jill thought. She should know her little prank got me in big trouble!

"Okay," Jill said, looking back at Ludmila and fighting tears. "Thanks for giving me a second chance."

"You are excused from practice this morning. This is time you should be using to get ready for Sectionals, which are in less than a week," Ludmila said. "Right now, I will work with skaters who value my time a little more."

"But Sectionals are important to me! I do value your time!" Jill cried.

"Then prove it to me this afternoon, and tomorrow, and every day before Sectionals, and every minute until you graduate from this Academy, Jill," Ludmila said. "And don't mess up. You are a talented skater. I'd hate to see you ruin your chances because you can't get to practice on time."

Jill nodded and hung her head. This was the worst thing that had ever happened to her. She turned and walked slowly back to Aspen House. Her parents had made so many sacrifices to send her here. Even with Jill's partial scholarship, the Academy was expensive. Her mom and dad would be heartsick if they found out Jill was on probation.

Inside the dorm, she paused in front of the big oak table in the common room. Lisa Welch always put the girls' mail there.

Jill spotted a pink envelope addressed to her. It was covered with skating stickers.

A letter from home, she thought, ripping it open. She flicked her eyes to the bottom of the letter to see which of her little brothers or sisters had written it. But it wasn't from home. It was from Kim, her Ice Pal.

Dear Jill,

Thank you for your letter. I am very excited to be your Ice Pal! I bet you are a great skater. I tried ice skating three times, before I got sick. It was fun. I fell down a lot! I did better on the third time.

Maybe someday you will give me lessons. If I get better. Right now the doctors say I can't skate for a while. I also can't take my dog, Buttons, for a walk. Buttons is very sad about this!

I really wish I could go to the Ice Pals show in Kansas City. I can't, though, because right now I'm in the hospital. Tomorrow I'm supposed to have an operation on my leg that might help me get better. But the doctors say I still won't be better in time to go to the Ice Pals show. I hear they will show it on cable TV. But I don't think we get Kansas City's cable stations here. I bet you will be the best skater there.

Please send me a picture of yourself. I want to put it in my Dream Book. I have been pasting pictures in my Dream Book for three years—since I was five years old. It's a regular notebook, but I put sparkle stickers on the front to make it look nice. I like stickers!

Inside my Dream Book I put pictures of stuff I want to see and do someday.

Some of the pictures:

The Empire State Building—because one day I am going to the top!

A chocolate rabbit as big as a person—I don't know where I can buy this but one day I am going to buy one and eat the whole thing in one day!

Some people in Italy stepping on grapes with their feet to make wine—I don't drink wine, but I want to try this. Maybe I can make grape juice this way.

A stegosaurus—I know these are not around anymore, but I still wish I could see one. My mom says the good thing about a dream is it can be about anything, even if it won't come true!

There are lots of other good things in my book. Maybe I can show it to you someday. I would like to meet you, so that's why I want a picture of you to put in my Dream Book, too!

Please, please write to me again. I loved your let-
ter. I keep it near my bed and I read it again every
night before I go to sleep.

                                    Love, your Ice Pal,
                                    Kim

Jill smiled. She carefully folded the letter and
tucked it back into the envelope. At least someone
thought she was wonderful—even if Ludmila didn't!

Kim seemed like such a sweet kid. The thought of
her being in the hospital was so sad. It made probation seem less terrible, somehow.

Jill ran upstairs and grabbed paper and a pen from
her desk. She flopped onto her bed and started to
write.

Dear Kim,

Thanks for writing! Your letter was great, too!
I'm really sorry that you can't come to the Ice Pals
show. I promise to write and tell you all about it.
Maybe you can see me skate some other time.
Meanwhile, here is a picture of me. I'm sorry it's
kind of blurry, but my little sister Randi took it
while I was skating, and I guess her hands moved. I
will try to get a better one to send you.

Your Dream Book sounds great. I would love to
see it someday. When I was little, most of my
dreams were about becoming a skater. I feel so
lucky that I have the chance to do what I always
wanted. Right now I am working even harder on

*my skating than usual. That's because I have an
important competition coming up soon—right after
the Ice Pals show!*

*The competition is in Irving, Texas, and it's
called Sectionals. The next step after Sectionals is
Nationals, and Nationals could even lead to a
place on the U.S. Olympic team! Still, I'm trying
not to be too nervous about Sectionals. It's hard to
skate well when you're nervous.*

*I hope everything goes really smoothly with your
operation. Someday, when you're feeling better, I'll
give you those skating lessons!*

Love, your Ice Pal,
Jill

Jill licked the envelope and put a stamp on it. She
pulled on her parka and walked out of Aspen House to
the mailbox at the bottom of the driveway.

She dropped the letter in and took a deep breath of
the cold, mountain air. She hoped Kim would like her
letter. Just sending it made her feel better.

But as Jill looked around at the quiet, snow-covered
campus, she realized it was deserted because everyone
was at practice. That's where I should be, too, she
thought bitterly. And if it wasn't for Carla, I would be.
Suddenly Jill didn't feel better at all. She had a feeling
she'd be using her free time before class thinking of
how she was going to get back at Carla!

9

Ludmila squinted through the glass of the windshield at the flat, green fields around them. "Well, girls, the turnoff for Kansas City should be coming up."

"Oh, good!" Carla bounced a little in the front seat. "I can't wait to see the arena. I'm really excited about the Ice Pals show tomorrow."

"I, for one, can't wait to get out of this van," Ludmila commented. "Driving for nine hours straight isn't easy. And we'll have another long drive ahead of us the day after the show."

"How far is it from Kansas City to Irving, Texas?" Jill asked from the backseat.

"About five hundred miles," Ludmila answered. "But we have to drive over the Ozark Mountains, so that will take extra time. We can make the trip in about ten hours, if we take some shortcuts and don't make too many stops. That will get you both to Irving just in time to get a good night's sleep before Sectionals start the next day.''

"I wish little Kim could make it to the show tomorrow," Jill said. "I tried to call her at the hospital today to let her know that I would be thinking about her. But her mom answered the phone and said Kim was sleeping."

"I think it's wonderful that you girls got involved in this program," Ludmila commented. "I bet it really made a big difference to those children."

"Oh, I know," Carla agreed. "Little Timmy must have been so happy to hear from me."

"You mean you finally wrote him a letter?" Jill asked.

"Of *course* I wrote to him," Carla snapped back. "I sent him a great big get-well card *and* a box of candy."

"Actually, Carla, are you sure he can eat candy?" Jill asked.

"What are you talking about? All kids love candy!" Carla said.

"Well, it's just that a lot of these kids are probably on special diets because they're sick," Jill explained.

"Since when do you know so much about sick kids?" Carla said grouchily.

"Since I did this whole Ice Pals project all by myself!" Jill snapped.

"Girls, please. Stop arguing." Ludmila peered through the windshield again. "Can one of you check the map? I'm almost certain our exit should have come up by now."

"*I'll* check it," Carla volunteered. "I'm really good at reading maps." She began to search the front seat. "Where is it?"

"It's back here." Jill reached for the Missouri map beside her on the seat. "I'll check."

"I said *I'd* check," Carla objected.

"I know, but I'm the one who found the map," Jill pointed out. She began to unfold it. "What road are we on, Ludmila?"

"Highway Forty-five," Carla answered authoritatively. "I know *exactly* where we are. Just give me the map, Jill."

"Actually, we're on Highway Forty," Ludmila corrected. "And *somebody*, please look at the map right away."

"I found Forty," Jill announced. "What exit do we want, Ludmila?"

"Give me that!" Carla snatched at the map. "I can do this!"

"Carla! I had it first!" Jill held tight to the map, but Carla kept pulling. There was a ripping sound.

"Carla!" Jill yelled.

"Jill, you did it!" Carla yelled back.

"Girls, please!" Ludmila slowed the van, pulled to the side of the road, and stopped. She twisted in her seat, an angry expression on her face. "What is this all about?"

"It's Jill's fault." Carla pouted. "She wouldn't give me the map."

"I had it first!" Jill objected.

"Stop it now! You sound like two little children fighting over a toy!" Ludmila's voice was stern. "You two are on your way to a charity event where you'll be representing the Academy. Then you are going to one of the most important competitions in your careers. This is no way to behave. Now, give me the map, please—or what's left of it."

The following evening, Jill stood in the dressing room at the Kansas City Civic Center with the other Ice Pals skaters. She checked herself in the mirror. She was wearing her favorite skating outfit—a short, black sequined dress with red sleeves and a black chiffon skirt. Her long black hair was braided down her back and tied with a red ribbon.

Jill glanced over at Carla, who was tightening her skate laces. Carla looked beautiful in her pink lace skating dress trimmed with silver rhinestones. Seeing Carla, Jill couldn't help feeling nervous. Even though Jill knew that the Ice Pals show wasn't supposed to be a competition, it was important to her to do well here. The arena was packed, and the cable station had set up cameras everywhere. Jill and Carla were representing the Ice Academy. Jill wanted to make sure she skated well.

The manager of the show knocked on the dressing-room door. "Okay, girls, we're starting in five minutes."

A ripple of excitement went through the dressing room. Jill joined the line of skaters filing out the door to the arena. There were fourteen skaters: six other female singles skaters, two male singles skaters, two sets of pairs, and Jill and Carla. Jill was scheduled to skate fourth, right after Carla.

The show opened with one of the pairs, a cute auburn-haired couple from Nebraska. They made Jill think of her friend Haley and Haley's partner, Patrick, back at Silver Blades. They both had red hair, too. Jill always thought their physical similarities added something special to their partnership on the ice.

Jill warmed up her muscles and watched from the boards as the Nebraska pair performed their lively routine. When they finished, the crowd exploded with applause.

"They were pretty good," Carla commented as she warmed up at Jill's side. "But she could have gotten a little more height on that last jump. Isabelle Lynch and Luke Hollenbeck from Blade Runners are better."

The next skater was a girl about Jill and Carla's age from a skating school in Minnesota. It was clear that she was enjoying her simple routine, but she didn't have Jill's or Carla's technical ability.

As the girl finished, Carla turned to Jill and rolled

her eyes. "Did you see that? What an amateur. A skater like that shouldn't even be allowed in a show like this."

"Remember, Carla, these skaters weren't chosen just for their skating ability. The show is *supposed* to be for *all* the Ice Pals coordinators," Jill pointed out. "Maybe she did a lot of work for the program."

Carla shrugged. "That still doesn't mean she can skate." Then she smiled. "Well, I'm up next. Time to show this crowd what *real* skating is all about."

Jill watched as Carla stepped onto the ice, skated confidently to the center, and struck her pose. The opening strains of the music began—a dramatic, melancholy violin piece. Carla launched into her routine with a series of back crossovers, going into some intricate footwork, varying sets of forward and back spirals, followed by a double axel.

Carla's skating was fast, strong, and precise as she came out of her double axel and stepped into a flying camel. She powered around the rink once more and lifted into a triple Lutz–double toe loop jump. Carla landed squarely and with ease, her smile never leaving her face.

Jill shifted uncomfortably in her spot at the boards. It was clear that Carla was skating her best. A hush had fallen over the other skaters as everyone watched her.

The tempo of the violin music picked up. Carla glided backward across the ice and shifted her weight. Jill knew what was coming next—a triple toe loop–

double loop combination. Carla executed it perfectly, getting a lot of height on the triple toe and going right into the double loop. She finished the combination gracefully, her face tilted toward the audience. Even Jill was spellbound. It had been an incredible skating performance.

Carla ended her routine with a dramatic series of Arabian cartwheels and flying splits and closed with a final scratch spin, her arms extended triumphantly.

The roar of the crowd was tremendous. Carla posed at the center of the ice for several minutes as the audience cheered.

"Wow!" a skater standing near Jill commented. "She's incredible. Do you know who she is?"

"I sure do. She's my roommate," Jill answered glumly.

Carla stepped off the ice, her face flushed. She shot Jill a smile. "Not bad, huh?" she said. "Wait till I tell Jesse. He'll be so proud of me." She smiled mysteriously. "He'll just be sad he wasn't here to give me my congratulatory kiss in person."

Jill stared at her. "Your *what*?"

But Carla kept smiling. Jill heard her name announced, but she couldn't move. She felt as if she were frozen in place.

Carla raised her eyebrows. "Excuse me, Jill, but I think they're calling your name. Although, I have to say, I don't blame you for not wanting to go on after the performance I just gave."

A hush had settled over the arena. Jill heard her

name announced again. She forced her legs to move in the direction of the ice.

Jill skated to the center of the ice, still feeling numb. What was Carla talking about? Did Carla really think that Jesse would have kissed her if he'd been here? Could that mean that Jesse had kissed Carla *before*?

That meant everything Jill had done to follow Veronica's advice and ignore Jesse had failed! For the past week, Jill had dodged Jesse on the way to classes and practice. She had sat with other people in the dining hall. And she had told Jesse she was rushing to get somewhere whenever he tried to talk to her. But instead of making Jesse ask her to the dance, Jill's behavior had obviously just made him like Carla even more!

As the first strains of Jill's lively music began, she realized that she hadn't even struck her opening pose. She hurried to catch up with the music, lurching into the back crossovers that started her routine. Focus, Jill reminded herself. You've got to focus on your skating now. Forget about Jesse and Carla.

But she couldn't get Carla's words about the kiss— or Carla's smiling face—out of her mind. As Jill sprang into her double axel, she realized that she was totally off balance. The jump was normally an easy one for Jill, but she had started out completely off center. She lost her balance, and, to her horror, she landed on the ice with a thud.

Jill quickly picked herself up off the ice and hurried into the rest of her routine. How could I have fallen on a *double axel*? she asked herself in shock. Now she was dreading the rest of her routine. If she couldn't make the double axel, how was she going to complete the more demanding parts? And what about Sectionals? She couldn't expect to place with a performance like the one she was giving now.

Just forget about everything and make it through this routine, Jill told herself as she sped around the ice, gathering momentum. It's only an exhibition. It doesn't have to be perfect. Just get through it.

The next jump was supposed to be a triple salchow–double toe loop combination, but Jill was afraid to go for it. At the last minute, she reduced the triple salchow to a double. She felt so ashamed of her performance. She wished the routine were over.

Finally it was time for the last jumps of her routine, a triple flip and double toe loop. Jill barely made it through the triple flip, landing shakily and getting a bad start on the double toe. After a shaky second landing, Jill wobbled into her final sit spin to end the routine. She stared down at the ice.

The audience applauded politely. But Jill knew she had performed terribly. She had humiliated herself in front of Carla and the other skaters, in front of the whole Civic Center, and in front of all those television cameras. She wished she had never come to Kansas City!

10

"Last night was the greatest!" Carla exclaimed happily. "Did you hear all that applause? Wow, my first solo performance for cable television, and they loved me! I'm so glad I decided to be part of Ice Pals!"

"You performed very well, Carla," Ludmila said without taking her eyes off the steep, curving road.

Jill turned her head and stared out the window of the van. They were driving through the Ozark Mountains toward Texas. Rugged peaks and rocky cliffs surrounded them. Dark storm clouds rolled overhead, and raindrops were beginning to patter on the windshield. The weather matched Jill's mood perfectly.

Carla leaned forward in the backseat. "Didn't you think it was fun, Jill?"

"Not *exactly*," Jill replied in a low voice.

"Oh, that's right, I forgot about your fall," Carla

said, giggling. "I guess that double axel *can* be kind of rough. Maybe you'll be able to land it tomorrow at Sectionals."

Jill whipped around. "Why don't you just leave me alone, Carla! You know I can do a double axel with no problem at all!"

"Girls, that's enough," Ludmila said, gripping the steering wheel tightly. "Jill, we all have our difficult days. What's important now is getting yourself back on track for tomorrow."

"I was just joking around a little," Carla said, pouting. "Anyway, even if I *hadn't* skated beautifully, I'd still feel proud of the way I helped those poor little sick kids with my performance."

"Oh, *right*," Jill muttered as the van rounded another sharp bend. "Like you really care about those kids, Carla."

"What's that, Jill?" Carla's voice was sharp.

"You don't care about those kids at all," Jill shot back. "If you did, you would have helped me organize the Ice Pals project from the beginning. I had to sign up *every* student at the Academy. Every single one! And I had to make sure they wrote their letters so those sick kids wouldn't wait for something that never came! You didn't lift a finger!"

"I *did* help," Carla said. "I helped as much as I possibly could. It just so happened I had a ton of really important other things to do, too." She paused. "Like work on getting *my* skating routine right for the show," she added.

"Like picking out a theme for the formal, you mean! Being president of the decorating committee was obviously a lot more important to you than anything for Ice Pals," Jill said accusingly. "You only cared about Ice Pals because it meant you got to be in the show and on television!"

"It's a good thing I *was* in the show," Carla responded. "*Somebody* had to skate well and represent the Academy!"

"Girls! I can't concentrate! Be quiet!" Ludmila said. She slowed the van to steer around a sharp bend. Suddenly the pattering rain became a torrent. Ludmila speeded up the wipers and slowed the van even more.

"Besides, the formal *is* important," Carla went on. "Maybe not to *you*, Jill. But it's going to be a very big night for me—and Jesse."

"What are you talking about?" Jill demanded. She turned around and glared at Carla. "Did Jesse ask you to go to the formal with him?"

"None of your business!" Carla shot back. "Who do you think you are, Jill? You don't *own* Jesse, you know!"

"I said, *that is enough!*" Ludmila cried. She turned the wheel sharply to avoid an oncoming car, and the van lurched. "You two have done nothing but argue since we left, and I'm tired of it. It is not the way I expect skaters from the Academy to behave." She leaned forward and swiped angrily at the inside of the windshield where it was fogging up. "I can hardly see in this rain—and right now I wonder if it's worth it," she muttered.

Jill hung her head and picked at an imaginary piece of thread on her jeans. It was bad enough that she had embarrassed herself in front of the entire Kansas City Civic Center. Now Ludmila was upset and disappointed in her again. It seemed as if all Jill did lately was fail Ludmila!

"I don't expect you two to be best friends," Ludmila went on as the van began to climb a steep, narrow incline.

"Good," Carla whispered from the backseat.

Jill scowled at Carla.

"But I *do* expect you to learn to get along," Ludmila said.

A heavy silence fell over the van.

Ludmila just doesn't understand the way Carla is, Jill thought. She doesn't know how Carla's always trying to make herself look good and me look bad. She doesn't have to live with Carla!

Ludmila glared at Carla in the rearview mirror and then directed an equally stern expression at Jill.

"At the very least, I expect you to keep it down for the rest of this trip," she said. "I'm tired. I've been behind the wheel for five and a half hours today, and we still have several hours to go. Driving these winding mountain roads isn't easy, and it takes all my concentration to—"

Just then Jill spotted something up ahead. A huge

truck—so huge that it was taking up more than its own lane—and it was heading straight for them!

"Ludmila!" Jill screamed, pointing out the windshield. "Watch out!"

Ludmila snapped her head forward and yanked the van's steering wheel to the right. The truck rumbled by, its oversized tires throwing a spray of water onto the van's windshield. As the wipers cleared the water away, Jill gasped. The road curved sharply to the left—but the van was moving straight—toward the brightly painted guardrail!

Ludmila swung the steering wheel hard to the left, trying to make the sharp turn. The tires screeched on the wet road. The van began sliding sideways with a sickening jolt, heading toward the guardrail—and toward the steep, rocky hill that lay beyond it.

Carla screamed. Jill heard a cracking, wrenching sound as the van slammed through the rail.

11

Suddenly everything in the van was moving.

Suitcases crashed against the walls. Papers flew through the air. Jill saw patches of rainy sky, then rocky ground. Her arms and legs flapped around like a rag doll's as the van pounded the ground again and again. She felt her head smack the window next to her.

There was a series of loud bangs.

The engine whined.

Somebody screamed.

Finally, after what seemed like forever, the van slammed onto the ground one final time and slid slowly to a stop.

Jill was wedged against the door. She lay still, dazed.

The van was silent, except for a few quiet clicking sounds from the engine. It wasn't running anymore.

Slowly Jill raised her head, trying to move. She was still buckled into her seat, but something felt terribly wrong. The stick shift was digging into her left thigh. Her head was hanging down. She felt as if she was about to slide into the driver's side.

A loud wail came from the back of the van. It was Carla. "Help! Help! Somebody help!"

"Carla!" Jill's voice was trembling.

"Jill! What happened?" Carla sounded as terrified as Jill felt.

"I'm not sure," Jill responded. "Are you okay?"

"I think so," Carla replied. "Are you?"

"I guess so," Jill said. She turned her head to look out the passenger window. There was nothing in sight—no road, no trees, no truck. Nothing but the fading gray of the sky. The rain was still coming down, but it wasn't as heavy. For a moment Jill just stared. Why was she seeing the sky? she wondered.

Then Jill realized what had happened. The tumbling van had stopped on its side. The passenger side was up in the air, and the driver's side—Ludmila's side—was on the ground!

Quickly Jill turned to Ludmila.

The small woman was lying against the driver's-side door. The window behind her head was cracked in a spiderweb pattern.

Jill gasped. "Oh, no! Ludmila, are you okay?"

"What's going on?" Carla wailed. "What happened to Ludmila?"

"I think she's hurt!" Jill cried. "Ludmila, are you okay?" She reached down and gripped Ludmila's arm.

Ludmila let out a groan. "Ooh. My head!"

"We have to get out of here!" Carla yelled. "I want to get out!"

"The van's on its side," Jill said. She braced her legs on the driver's seat and unbuckled her seat belt. Reaching her arm behind her, she tugged at the door handle. The door was stuck shut.

"I can't budge this. What about your door, Carla? Will it open?"

"I'll try," Carla answered. Jill could hear her fidgeting with the handle of the sliding door. "I can't get it!"

"Try again, Carla," Jill said. "Try harder."

"I *can't*!" Carla's voice cracked.

Jill felt panic rise up in her. What if we're trapped? she thought desperately.

"Hold on! I'm coming back there, Carla," Jill said. She squeezed her way between the driver's seat and the passenger seat. She and Carla were both crouching on the side window that was now on the ground.

Together the girls tried to force open the door. Jill felt a searing pain in her shoulder as she pushed against the handle.

Suddenly the door creaked and rolled open. Cold raindrops swept into the van.

"We did it!" Carla cried. "Let's get out of here."

"You go first, Carla," Jill said. "Ludmila, can you hear me?"

Ludmila let out a low groan. "Okay, Ludmila, just hold on," Jill said, trying to hide the worry in her voice. "As soon as I'm out, I'll try to open the front passenger door from the outside. We'll pull you through that way."

"Do you really think that's going to work?" Carla asked.

Ludmila let out another groan.

"We have to at least *try*!" Jill cried. She looked down and saw that her hands were shaking.

"All right. Don't yell," Carla said. "I'm just—I'm really scared, okay?"

"Me too," Jill said.

Carla climbed through the open door. Then Jill hoisted herself through and jumped down onto the rocky ground. As she did, she felt another stab of pain in her left shoulder. Jill held on to the side of the van and straightened up slowly. Her body ached and felt cold, but she was sure nothing was broken.

She looked at Carla. A large welt was beginning to form on the other girl's forehead, and there were tears in her eyes.

For a moment they stared at each other. Jill knew she and Carla were thinking the same thing: I'm glad to be alive.

Carla's eyes glanced away and then widened.

"Oh no!" Carla shrieked. "Look!"

Jill turned and saw that the van had come to rest halfway down the hill. It was lying on its side on a small flat space. But dirt was crumbling away beneath the van. Rocks were bouncing wildly down the hill. A wide, rushing river roared along the base of the hill.

"We've got to get Ludmila out right away!" Jill responded. "The van could slide down into the river!"

The girls heard another moan from Ludmila inside the van.

"Help me!" Ludmila said. "I can't move my leg!"

"I'm coming, Ludmila!" Jill called. She pulled herself onto the van's front wheel and began tugging hard at the dented front door.

"I'll help," Carla said. She climbed up and put her hand on top of Jill's.

"Ready? Pull!" Jill said.

Together the girls tugged at the door as hard as they could. It finally gave, with a loud screech of metal.

"We did it," Jill said. She jumped down and leaned into the open passenger door.

"Ludmila! Give me your hands and I'll pull you out!" Jill called.

Carla crowded next to Jill at the door to the van. "*I'll* help you, too, Ludmila!"

Ludmila turned her head slowly toward them and groaned. It scared Jill to see her coach looking so helpless. She felt Carla shivering next to her. The rain had almost stopped, but both girls were cold and wet.

"Ludmila, try to unbuckle your seat belt. Then come this way a little on your own first," Jill instructed.

Ludmila seemed groggy. But she managed to nod to show she understood. Jill watched as Ludmila fumbled with her seat belt and finally managed to unbuckle it.

She slowly pulled herself up toward the passenger door. Her eyes were glazed, and her face was twisted in pain.

Jill and Carla leaned into the van. They both reached for Ludmila's arms. Jill ignored her aching shoulder.

"Carla!" Jill said. "Move over. I can't reach Ludmila while you're crowded in here."

"You get out!" Carla said, shoving at Jill. "I'm stronger."

Jill stretched farther until she could reach Ludmila's arm. Carla grabbed Ludmila's sweater. They both started pulling.

Ludmila moaned and cried out. "Stop! Stop! You're hurting me!"

Frustrated, Jill eased up on Ludmila's arm.

"We have to be careful," she said, gritting her teeth. "We could hurt Ludmila even worse."

"I *am* being careful," Carla shot back. "You're the one who grabbed her too hard."

Ludmila slowly twisted her body until her feet were under her. Jill and Carla gently pulled her toward the open door. Finally the girls managed to haul Ludmila out of the van.

Pale and shaking, Ludmila hobbled a step. Then she collapsed on the dirt.

Jill and Carla quickly knelt next to her.

"Ludmila, are you okay?" Carla asked.

Ludmila shook her head slowly. "My ankle. I think it's—it's broken," she managed to say. She put her hand to her head and winced. "My head hurts so much!" When Ludmila withdrew her hand, it was bright red.

"She's *bleeding*!" Carla cried.

Jill dug through her pocket and found a tissue. She pulled it out and pressed it to the gash on Ludmila's head.

"We need to clean it so it doesn't get infected," Jill said. "I know! I have water in the van!"

"I'll get it!" Carla stood up and pushed past Jill.

"I'll get it," Jill argued. "You don't even know where it is, Carla."

"I'm closer!" Carla insisted. She started climbing into the van.

"Oh, go ahead," Jill muttered. She knelt down again next to Ludmila.

Carla rattled around in the van, searching for the water. Jill heard a loud echoing sound.

A large rock had come loose from under the van and it was bouncing downhill. Dirt was rapidly crumbling away from under the side of the van. Suddenly the van groaned and rocked slightly.

"Carla!" shrieked Jill. "Get out!"

"We need water," Carla's muffled voice called.

"Carla! Get out now! I think the van's going to fall!" Jill screamed.

Carla's startled face peered over the edge of the sliding door.

"Get out!" Jill said, reaching toward her. "Hurry!"

"I can't," Carla croaked. "My foot is stuck."

The van slid another inch.

"Oh no! Help me, Jill!" Carla screamed. Jill could see Carla's head bob as she yanked at her leg.

"Carla!" Jill cried. She hesitated, then hurled herself into the van.

Jill slid down the backseat, resting her weight on her arms. She could see that Carla's leg was caught between a suitcase and the front seat. She pushed the case as hard as she could. Carla tugged at her foot frantically.

The van slid several more inches.

Jill could hear rocks cascading down the steep hill and splashing into the wild river below.

"I still can't move it!" Carla screamed, pulling her leg.

Jill took a deep breath and pushed the case again. It gave half an inch. Suddenly Carla's leg popped free, and she pushed herself up and out of the van.

The van slid another few inches and then started picking up speed. Jill scrabbled backward. She felt Carla grab her from behind and pull her out of the sliding van. The two girls fell to the ground, just as the van tilted downward sharply.

They watched as the van disappeared over the edge.

12

There was a loud crash, followed by silence. Jill and Carla stood up and peered down to the bottom of the hill.

The van had smashed into a large tree and come to a stop near the edge of the river.

Jill's stomach sank. She and Carla had almost been in that van when it fell. Suitcases, clothes, and papers were scattered in its path.

Far above, Jill could just see the top of the hill they had hurtled down. She strained her ears, but she couldn't hear any passing traffic.

The rain had finally stopped, and the sun had come out, but it would set soon. Jill was already so cold she was shivering. Ludmila sat in the dirt several yards away. Her eyes were unfocused, and she was pressing the bloody wad of tissue to her forehead.

"Oh, great. How are we ever going to get out of here?" Carla said miserably. "And all my stuff is down there."

Ludmila let out another moan. Jill turned and saw that her coach had buried her head in her arms. She ran back and knelt next to her. Ludmila reached out, and Jill gripped her hand.

"Maybe one of us should hike up to the road," Jill said. "And then get a ride to the nearest town and bring back help."

"You mean *you* should hike up to the road, right?" Carla responded, shivering and clutching herself. "Well, forget it. By the time you get back, the sun will be down. No way am I waiting on this freezing cold, dark mountain while you go riding off to the next town."

Jill didn't like the idea of waiting alone with Ludmila, either. Who knew what kind of animals might come out after dark? Even worse, what if Ludmila got even sicker, or—Jill wouldn't let herself think the worst.

"Maybe we could cover Ludmila with our coats and build her a fire, and then we could both hike up to the road," Carla said.

"No way!" Jill said. "We're not leaving Ludmila alone."

"Well, then, we could kind of prop Ludmila up between us and help her walk," Carla replied.

Jill turned and gazed up the mountain. "The road's

pretty far up," she remarked. "It's a steep climb. It would be hard to help Ludmila make it up."

"But we don't have a choice," Carla wailed. "We have to get out of here or we're never going to make it to Sectionals!"

Jill turned from where she was kneeling next to Ludmila.

"*Sectionals?*" Jill said. "You're worried about *Sectionals*? Ludmila is hurt. And we're stuck on a mountain and it's getting dark and cold and you're worried about *Sectionals*?"

Carla sniffed and wiped her nose.

"I'm scared for Ludmila, too, you know. But I also don't see what's so wrong with wanting to get to Sectionals. Maybe skating in some stupid exhibition and falling on your double axel is good enough for you, but it's not good enough for me. I've been skating my whole life so I can win Sectionals, and then Nationals. And then I'm going to skate in the Olympics and win a gold medal. And nothing is going to stop me!" By the time she was done, she was almost screaming. Her face was bright red and her green eyes were flashing. Her blond hair was flat and stringy from the rain. The welt on her forehead was an ugly red.

Jill stared at her in silence for a moment. "Carla," she said, "if you want to get to the Olympics, you have to get off this stupid hill first. And you're not getting off it without me and Ludmila. We have to work together. For once, you're not doing a solo, okay?"

Carla wiped her arm across her face. "You know, Jill, I'm not as selfish as you think," she said. "I don't want to leave Ludmila here, either."

"Then let's think of a plan," Jill said.

Suddenly Ludmila sat up straight and started speaking loudly in a language the girls didn't recognize.

"Ludmila!" Jill cried, running over to her. "Are you okay?"

"She must be speaking Russian," Carla said worriedly.

"I'm afraid she might be going into shock," Jill said. "We have to get her warm somehow. But with what?"

"Maybe I could go down to the van and get our coats," said Carla.

"Forget it," Jill said. "The hill's too steep. You could fall trying to climb down there. We've got to get Ludmila up the hill—now."

"I could hike up the hill and flag down a car," Carla said.

"I don't think there's time. We have to get Ludmila to a hospital right away. If you go alone, we'll have to wait for you to come back down with help. I think we should bring her up now."

"But how are we going to get Ludmila up the hill? She can't walk."

Suddenly Ludmila slumped over.

Jill bent down and cradled Ludmila. The coach's face was white, and her eyes were rolled back into her head. "Ludmila? *Ludmila!*" Jill screamed. "Answer me!"

13

"**W**hat should we do?" Carla asked, kneeling next to Ludmila.

"I don't know!" Jill cried.

"Let's see if she's breathing."

"Maybe I can find her pulse," Jill said shakily. She tried to remember what she had learned in health class back in Seneca Hills.

Jill groped for Ludmila's arm. She pulled up Ludmila's sleeve and pressed her fingers to the inside of her wrist.

"Do you feel anything?" Carla asked.

Jill paused, waiting. Please, please, Ludmila, be all right, she begged silently. Jill's own hand was shaking so hard, she couldn't feel anything at first.

Then, finally, Jill felt a faint throbbing inside Ludmila's wrist. Jill glanced quickly at Carla and nod-

ded. "Her pulse is still there. Maybe she just fainted."
She turned to Ludmila.

"Ludmila? Ludmila, can you hear me?" There was
no response.

Carla tapped Ludmila on the shoulder. "Ludmila?"
Carla's voice sounded frantic.

Jill's heart pounded. She squeezed Ludmila's hand
hard. "Ludmila, please! Ludmila, wake up!"

"What if she can't? What if she *never* wakes up?"
Carla cried.

Jill took a deep breath. "Carla, we have to figure out
a way to get her out of here."

"But what are we supposed to do?" Carla cried miserably.

"There has to be a way out of this. And it's up to us
to figure it out." Jill fixed her eyes on Carla's. "We can
do this, Carla. Together we can do this."

Carla shifted her gaze to the ground. "Okay. You're
right, Jill. We can do it. But what should we do?"

Jill thought for a moment. "If there was only some
way we could make something to carry Ludmila
with," she said.

Carla's eyes lit up. "You mean, like a stretcher?
That's a great idea!"

Jill sighed. "Sure, but what are we supposed to
make it out of?" She gazed around dejectedly.
"There's nothing out here but rocks and dirt."

"What about the stuff down in the van?" Carla suggested. "Maybe there's something there we could
use."

"I guess one of us has to try to climb down there and look around," Jill said.

"I'll do it," Carla said. "You stay with Ludmila." She jumped up. "I'll bring anything I see that might help us."

"Be careful, Carla," Jill called as Carla scrambled down the hill.

Jill turned back to Ludmila. Her eyes were half shut, and her mouth was slightly open. Jill stroked Ludmila's face and held her hand. "It's going to be okay, Ludmila. We're going to get you out of here," she said, hoping Ludmila could hear her.

A moment later, Jill heard Carla call her name from the bottom of the hill. She stood up and saw Carla waving to her.

"Jill! Come on! I need your help!" Carla called.

Jill glanced at Ludmila once more. She didn't want to leave her.

Carla called her again. "Jill! Come *on*!"

Jill hesitated. She peeled off her sweater and laid it over her coach.

"I have to leave you for a minute but I'll be right back," Jill said. "Don't worry," she added. "We're going to make a stretcher and carry you out of here."

Jill started climbing down the steep hill.

"Go to your left," Carla shouted from below. "There's an easy way to get down there."

Jill edged along a ledge and found what looked like a narrow, twisting path. She climbed down it slowly, grabbing on to big rocks that jutted out of the hillside. Finally she reached the van.

"Jill, I have an idea!" Carla said. "But I need your help."

"Okay, what is it?" Jill asked.

"There's a rug in the back of the van," Carla explained. "You know, in that space behind the back-seats where the luggage goes. I was thinking that we could carry Ludmila in that."

"Or even wrap her up in it! Yes!" Jill said.

"The problem is that it's stapled down or something," Carla said.

"Let's check it out," Jill said. "Maybe we can pull it up."

Carla climbed up on the van's front wheel and reached for the sliding door.

"No, Carla, this way!" Jill headed around the back of the van. "There's a hatch door back here." Jill felt for the release button and pressed it. The rear door of the van opened slightly. Jill and Carla managed to pull it open enough to crawl into the back of the van.

A blue speckled carpet covered the luggage area of the van.

"This should be just about big enough for Ludmila to lie on," Jill declared.

"*If* we can get it out of the van," Carla reminded her.

Jill dug at the edge of the carpet with her fingernails. "I think it's glued."

Carla joined Jill, pulling at the edge of the carpet. After a few minutes, Jill was panting. She could feel herself sweating, and her shoulder was aching more than ever. But the carpet was finally coming up. With a final rip, the girls tore the carpet free. Carla climbed out first. When Jill pushed through the door, she saw Carla pick something up from the ground.

Carla stood and waved a small package. "Skate laces," she said. "They could come in handy."

The two girls picked up the carpet and started up the hill.

"Wait," Jill said, stopping. "Once Ludmila is in the carpet, how are we going to carry it? We'll need handles or something." She looked back at the van. The metal of its roof rack sparkled under the last rays of the setting sun. Attached to the rack was a large nylon net to hold suitcases.

"Carla! Maybe we can use that net to help carry Ludmila once she's wrapped in the rug!" Jill dropped her end of the carpet and ran back to the van.

The net was perfect—strong enough for a heavy load, and large.

"It's just what we need," Jill said. "The only problem is getting it off the van. We don't have anything to cut it with."

Carla frowned, then gasped. "Yes we do!"

"We do?" Jill repeated.

"Jill, don't tell me you've actually forgotten the name of your old skating club!" Carla said.

"My old skating club?" Jill was confused. "We don't have time for games. What are you talking about, Carla?"

"Silver Blades," Carla replied. "Silver *Blades*!"

"Our *skates*! We could try to cut the net with our skate blades," Jill said. "Good idea, Carla. Do you think it will work?"

"It might," Carla said.

She crawled into the van and emerged a minute later holding a pair of skates. She removed the guards and handed one of the skates to Jill.

Jill grabbed the first string of tough nylon and started sawing at it. The skate blade kept slipping. Finally Jill used its ridged toe pick to slice through the nylon.

By the time they were done, Jill's hand was aching, and blisters were already forming on her palm.

"Done," Carla said from her side. She tossed her part of the net in Jill's direction. Jill scooped it up. Then she and Carla grabbed the carpet and struggled up the hill, back toward Ludmila.

Their coach was still unconscious when the girls got there. They put the net down and laid the carpet over it.

Carla bit her lip. "Okay, now how do we get her on it?"

"We have to lift her," Jill replied. "Let's start with her arms."

Jill took hold of one of Ludmila's wrists, and Carla picked up the other. Jill was amazed at how heavy the tiny woman was. Even with Carla helping, it was a struggle to slide Ludmila's upper body onto the rug.

"Okay," Jill panted. "Now let's do the same thing with her legs."

Jill reached for Ludmila's left leg.

"Careful of her ankle!" Carla reminded her.

"Oh, right." Jill planted her hands on Ludmila's knee and carefully bent it, cradling Ludmila's injured ankle as best she could with her upper arms. Ludmila had no way to tell them if they were hurting her, Jill realized.

They slid Ludmila's hips and legs onto the carpet.

Jill rolled the carpet over Ludmila, but it sprang open.

"We need something to hold it closed," Jill declared. "Those laces you brought!"

"Good idea!" Carla said, pulling them from her pocket. They tied the laces together so they would be long enough to wrap around the carpet. When they were done, the carpet was wrapped snugly around Ludmila.

Jill gazed around. The sun had set completely. The clouds had cleared from the sky. A full, bright moon lit the hillside.

"Well, at least with that moon we can see which way to go."

"Oh, don't worry, we know which way to go," Carla commented. "The hardest way—up. You ready?"

Jill nodded. She took hold of the net near Ludmila's head. Carla grabbed the end near her feet.

"She's heavy," Carla moaned.

"She is," Jill said. "But we don't have a choice."

The girls climbed in silence for several minutes. The only sounds were rocks sliding under their feet and their heavy breathing as they struggled with their load.

"Let's rest for a second," Carla finally gasped.

They set Ludmila down gently on a grassy, flat spot.

"Jill," Carla said. "There's something I want to tell you. Remember when you were late the other morning? And Ludmila was really mad at you?"

"Yes?" Jill said.

"Well . . . I kind of turned your alarm off," Carla said, looking down at the ground. "I did it just as a joke. I didn't know you'd get in such big trouble."

Jill shook her head. "Forget about it."

"I'll tell Ludmila what I did," Carla said. "That is, if . . . I mean, *when* we get out of here. And I'll tell her how you saved me when my foot was stuck in the van."

"You pulled me out of the van, too, Carla," Jill reminded her. "Somehow, after all this, I don't really care about that stupid alarm clock anymore. Come on. We'd better get going." The girls lifted Ludmila and kept climbing.

Twenty minutes later, Jill was breathing hard with exhaustion. She and Carla were almost at the top of the ravine. Now Jill could make out the empty road directly above them in the moonlight. The girls hadn't heard one car in the entire time they had struggled to pull Ludmila up the hill.

Just as Jill was wondering how to get Ludmila to a hospital, she heard a rumbling sound.

Carla turned to her. "What's that?"

Jill fixed her eyes on the road. She saw the glare of two headlights rounding a bend in the road. "A car!"

"Hurry!" Carla cried, picking up her pace.

Jill shook her head. "We'll never make it in time. Even if one of us tries to run. The car has practically passed us already."

Jill and Carla watched in dejected silence as the headlights swung by on the road above them.

"Maybe there'll be another one soon," Carla said hopefully.

"Yeah, maybe," Jill responded.

"Well, then, I say let's make sure we're up there by the time there is." Carla picked up her pace.

Jill sighed. Her shoulder was throbbing. She was tired, cold, frustrated, and scared. And hungry, now, too. But Carla was right. The sooner they got to the road, the better the chances for helping Ludmila.

Jill sped up her pace to match Carla's. Her hands were raw where she'd been holding Ludmila's stretcher. She could see the edge of the road above her. It's not really that far, Jill reasoned. Like climbing three flights of stairs, she told herself. Very steep stairs.

Jill kept her eyes on the ground, searching for the

most solid spots to place her feet. The ground was muddy, and there were loose rocks everywhere. Jill's wet sneakers slipped on a flat rock and she fell to her knees. She barely managed to keep from letting go of the stretcher.

"I'm okay," she said quickly. The two girls continued up. Finally, they neared the top. The road was only a few yards away. But this was also the steepest part of the hill. Jill put all her effort into climbing.

Then Jill heard a familiar rumbling sound. Jill and Carla both realized what it was.

"Another car!" the two girls cried out at once.

They hurried up the final yards of the hill as fast as they could. Jill could see the headlights approaching.

"Hurry!" Carla yelled. "We can't miss this one!"

They reached the top of the ravine—just as the car passed them and continued up the road.

"Stop!" Jill yelled. "Stop! Please, stop!"

14

Carla gently set down her end of the stretcher and began waving her arms. "Help! Help!"

Jill set down her end and watched the car's taillights continue along the road.

Then, miraculously, the car slowed down and stopped.

"They see us!" Jill felt a surge of relief as the car began backing down the road toward them.

The car pulled to a stop beside the two girls. A woman with shoulder-length black hair leaned over and rolled down the window on the passenger side. "Are you all right?"

"No! We need help!" Carla cried.

"We had an accident!" Jill blurted out. She turned and pointed back down the ravine. "Our van is down there."

The woman looked concerned. She opened her door and stepped out. "Are you girls alone?"

"No, we're with our coach," Jill explained. "Ludmila Petrova from the International Ice Academy in Denver."

The woman seemed confused. "Where is she?"

Jill pointed to the rolled-up carpet covered with netting at her feet. Ludmila's head was barely visible. "Right here. I think she's hurt pretty bad," Jill added.

The woman's eyes widened in shock. "Oh, my! Is she unconscious?"

"We think she fainted," Jill said.

The woman bent down beside Ludmila. "Can you hear me?" she called. Ludmila moaned.

"Let's get her into the car right away," the woman said. She opened a rear door. "We can lay her across the backseat. You two can sit up front with me."

The three of them hurried to lift Ludmila, still wrapped in her blanket of carpet, into the backseat. Jill and Carla squeezed into the front.

The woman stepped on the gas. "There's a small town about a half hour from here. We could use a phone there to call an ambulance," she said. "And you could call your school and tell them what happened."

"That's a good idea," Carla said. "We need to get to a phone as soon as possible. We have to find a way to get to Sectionals—that's a very important competition we're supposed to skate in."

Ludmila moaned in the backseat. The woman frowned.

"Maybe we should drive straight to a hospital," she said. "There's one in Oklahoma City, but it's about ninety miles."

"We should go to the hospital," Jill said.

"No! To a phone," Carla said.

Jill turned and glared at Carla. "What is wrong with you?" she said loudly. "You still don't understand anything! We need to get Ludmila to a hospital. Now!"

"I agree," the woman said. "I'll get you there as fast as I can."

"Thank you," Jill said with relief. "Thanks a lot."

Two hours later, Jill and Carla sat on the green plastic seats of the hospital waiting room. They had both been looked at by doctors. Jill's shoulder was bruised, but nothing was broken. The gash on Carla's head had been taped.

Jill stared at the swinging doors that led to the examining rooms. "What's taking those doctors so long?"

"I guess she must be hurt pretty badly," Carla commented.

A blond woman in a nurse's white uniform walked into the waiting room and smiled at the girls.

"Are you two here with Ms. Petrova?" the nurse asked.

Jill stood up quickly. "Yes, Ludmila Petrova. Is she going to be okay?"

"The doctors are still with her, but I think she's going to be just fine," the nurse responded. "She's got a fracture in that ankle and a pretty severe concussion. She probably lost consciousness because of the pain, but she's all right now. In fact, she seems more concerned about how you two are doing than she is about herself."

"You mean she's awake?" Carla said.

"Oh, yes, she came around a little while ago," the nurse answered. "And the first words out of her mouth were about you girls—Jill and Carla, right?"

"That's right," Jill answered. "Ludmila is our coach."

"Yes, I hear you're ice skaters," the nurse said. "Ms. Petrova tells me you were all on your way to an ice-skating competition in Texas when the accident happened."

"That's right," Carla responded. "Sectionals. It's a really important event." She lowered her head. "But I guess we're not going to make it there."

"That's what I came to talk to you about," the nurse continued. "Ms. Petrova has made arrangements for you both to travel on to Irving tomorrow. The Ice Academy is sending a hired car to take you there."

"You're kidding!" Carla jumped up. "You mean we get to go to Sectionals after all?"

"I can't believe it!" Jill exclaimed. Then she sighed. "But what about our skates and stuff? It's all back in the ravine with the van."

"The state police are on their way to retrieve the van and your luggage," the nurse explained. "Ms. Petrova won't be ready to travel with you, but she said to tell you that Simon Wells from the Academy will meet you there. Meanwhile, I'm going to show you a room here at the hospital where you can get some sleep."

"Can we see Ludmila?" Jill asked.

The nurse nodded and smiled. "But just for one minute," she warned. "And then we need to let her rest."

The nurse led them through the swinging doors to a curtained-off bed. Ludmila was propped up on some pillows. There was a bandage around her head, and Jill could make out a cast around Ludmila's leg under the sheet.

"Ludmila! You're okay!" Jill cried, a grin breaking over her face.

Ludmila winced at the loud noise, but she smiled back.

"Shhh!" the nurse whispered. "I'll be right back for you girls. Don't get your coach too excited!"

Jill and Carla stood on either side of the bed. Ludmila reached out and held their hands.

"Thank you, girls," she whispered. "I know you carried me up that hill."

"How did you know?" Jill said. "You were asleep the whole time."

"Not the whole time," Ludmila said. "I was drifting in and out of consciousness."

"You mean, you could hear us talking?" Carla said.

Ludmila squeezed Jill's hand. "I could hear you comforting me, Jill. It helped a great deal."

The nurse poked her head through the curtain. "Okay, girls. Let's go. You two could probably use some sleep, yourself."

"Good night, Ludmila," Jill and Carla both said. They started walking away.

"Girls," Ludmila said. "I won't be at Sectionals to coach you—so listen to Simon's instructions. I know you'll both do your best. Remember that, no matter what, to me you're both champions already. Now go to Texas and show everyone else what you can do. Bring home some medals for the Academy."

15

Jill pushed through the doors of the Irving Ice Arena with Carla beside her.

They had made it to Sectionals the day before, just in time to skate their short programs. Jill had performed badly—she had been tired and her bruised shoulder had ached. Worse, Simon hadn't left the Academy until the night before because of a snowstorm, so Jill and Carla had had no coach. Jill had finished in sixth place.

None of that had seemed to bother Carla, though. She had skated her short program beautifully, coming in second. No one ever would have known she'd been in a serious accident the day before.

Including me, Jill thought bitterly. Carla had gone back to being as unpleasant as ever, at the arena and in their hotel room.

Jill scanned the crowd, looking for Simon's tall figure and red hair. He had called the hotel and told the girls he would meet them at the arena today. Just then she heard a voice behind her. "Jill? Carla?" Jill turned and saw Simon waving and grinning at them.

"Simon!" Jill felt a rush of relief at seeing his familiar face.

"Girls!" Simon wrinkled his brow in concern. "Are you two all right?"

"I'm fine," Carla replied. "Fine and ready to skate!"

"That's good," Simon said. "I'm sorry I didn't get here in time for your short programs yesterday. After the airport in Denver got snowed in, I decided to drive. I was on the road all night and I just got here a few minutes ago."

"That's okay," Jill said. "I barely made it through my short program, though."

"I can certainly understand why, after what you've been through," Simon said. "But today's the real test, Jill. You and Carla have got to skate your long programs and those count for two-thirds of your score here. Are you both up to it?"

"I'm up to it, Simon," Carla said.

Jill just nodded.

"Well, you're both in the final grouping. Which means you've got to go change and warm up soon."

"I don't need a lot of time to get warmed up," Carla boasted. "I could probably go out there and skate perfectly right this second. But you definitely need to warm up, Jill. And be careful not to overdo it with your quadriceps stretches this time."

Jill shook her head. Carla would never change. And that meant she would always be nasty to Jill.

"Let's head over to your rooting section," Simon suggested. He smiled. "Once word got around that I was driving instead of flying, a lot of the kids at the Academy decided to come with me. They heard about your accident and wanted to come show their support."

Jill and Carla walked around the rink with Simon.

"How's Ludmila?" Simon asked Jill. "I spoke to her over the phone, but that's never the same as seeing someone in person."

"We didn't get to talk to her for very long," Jill said. "But she seemed okay. And the nurse told us Ludmila will be back in Colorado in a couple of days."

Jill spotted a large group of skaters from the Academy a few yards away. Jesse was there! Jill's heart leaped.

Jesse spotted Jill and waved. Jill turned her head away quickly. She couldn't bear to look at him, knowing that he liked Carla better.

"Hi, Jesse!" Jill heard Carla yell beside her. Carla waved and smiled at Jesse. Jill remembered what Carla had said about how Jesse would have kissed her if he'd been at the Ice Pals show. She felt a stab of jealousy.

Jesse headed toward them.

Carla sped up and cut in front of Jill. "Jesse, hi!"

"It sure is good to see you guys!" Jesse responded. "We were all really worried about you."

Carla put her hands on Jesse's shoulders. "Wait till I tell you all about it! It was incredible! Did you know that I actually had to *carry* Ludmila up the side of a mountain? I'm in excellent shape, though. I saved her life, you know!"

Jill turned and walked away. Carla was making it sound as if she had climbed up the ravine with Ludmila all by herself. And Jesse probably believed every word of it.

An hour later, Jill stepped onto the ice to begin her five-minute warm-up. She saw Carla across the rink. Carla was landing her jumps strongly, and her spins were precise and graceful. Jill's own movements felt stiff and jerky. She was still sore from the accident.

After several minutes, the skaters were told to leave the ice. Jill found a quiet place in a corridor behind the rink. As she did some light stretches to keep her muscles warm, she tried to focus on her routine. But she couldn't stop thinking about Jesse and Carla. Jill had always thought that her friendship with Jesse was special. But now, it was clear that Jesse liked Carla better.

Jill heard a burst of applause from the rink and

knew that the first skater in their group was going on. As she continued to stretch, she pictured Jesse and Carla dancing together at the formal, gazing into each other's eyes. The ceiling would be covered with silver stars, and the room would be filled with twinkling blue lights. It was supposed to be *Jill* who would be "dancing in the moonlight" with Jesse—not Carla!

Jill heard a muffled announcement and then Carla's name over the loudspeaker. Carla is skating to center ice right now, Jill thought. She heard Carla's music start. A few seconds later, she heard applause. Carla must have landed the first triple jump in her routine—and, from the sound of the clapping, she had done it with her usual grace and style.

I have to stop thinking about Jesse and Carla and focus on *my* skating, Jill told herself fiercely. Jill felt angry at herself for being jealous of Carla. But she realized it went deeper than that now. She thought Carla had become her friend—that something special had happened on the mountain. But the minute they were safe, Carla had gone back to her usual behavior.

Jill remembered her terrible performance three days before, at the Ice Pals show. I've been through so much since then, she thought. She was tired and sore, and her shoulder was tender. Jill was worried. Not just about her shoulder, but about everything. Her short program had been dismal. What if she wasn't up to skating her long program, which was even harder? If she didn't medal, she wouldn't make it to Nationals.

And if she didn't make it to Nationals, she could say good-bye to her Olympic dreams.

As Jill slid into a split, she felt a slight twinge in her thigh muscle. That's from that stupid stretching contest with Carla, she reminded herself. And Carla had seemed almost glad it had happened—she was still making mean remarks about it!

Jill heard another burst of applause from the rink. Carla must be skating perfectly, she thought bitterly. Jill wished Carla had pulled her quadricep muscle—so she would know how much it hurt. In fact, Jill thought, I wish Carla would fall down *now*—then she'll never make it to the Olympics!

An even louder round of applause drifted into the corridor. So much for that wish, Jill thought. She took a deep breath and sat back.

Suddenly Jill had a sickening thought. Her competition with Carla had made her just *like* Carla! She had stopped caring about the things that mattered—like sportsmanship, honor, and doing her best. All she wanted to do was beat Carla or get back at her. Now she was even wishing Carla would fall!

Jill pictured Carla standing on the mountain, saying that she was going to skate in the Olympics—even if it meant leaving Ludmila there.

Then a thought hit Jill like a lightning bolt. It didn't matter if Carla was the greatest skater, the prettiest girl, or the best flirt in the world. Jill didn't want to be like Carla. She wanted to be Jill Wong. Not the Jill Wong who was bitter and jealous of Carla Benson. Not the Jill Wong who followed stupid advice about playing hard to get. She wanted to be the Jill Wong who had a wonderful family and a good friend named Jesse, and who loved to skate more than anything in the world. She wanted to be the old Jill Wong!

Why should she compare herself to anyone, let alone Carla? The only person Jill had to compete with was herself. And the only dreams she had to follow were her own.

More applause exploded from the rink. Then Jill heard her name called over the loudspeaker. It was her turn to skate. Jill felt a surge of energy and excitement. She was still tired and sore, but she couldn't wait to get to her favorite place—the ice.

I've come this far, and nothing's going to stop me, she thought. I'm going to go out there and give the best performance I can.

16

Jill stepped onto the ice. She adjusted the skirt of her emerald green skating dress and glided smoothly to the center of the rink.

Her heart was pounding with anticipation as she struck her starting position, with her left skate behind her, toe pick resting on the ice, and her head turned dramatically over her right shoulder. The opening bars of her lively music began. As a drumbeat filled the air, she inhaled deeply. This is it, she told herself. The first step to your Olympic dream. Think about your skating and nothing else.

Launching into her back crossovers, she reminded herself to breathe smoothly and evenly. The first jump was the double axel, normally an easy one for her. It was also the jump she had fallen on at the Ice Pals exhibition.

Focus! she reminded herself. Picture your goal in your head. You've done this jump perfectly a thousand times. You can do it this time, too.

Jill landed the double axel with her usual ease and headed smoothly on to the triple salchow–double toe loop combination. Her strength wasn't what it usually was—she had to push hard to get enough lift. But she landed both jumps strongly.

Her confidence was returning, and she was beginning to enjoy herself. Nothing in the world felt as good as skating. She was happy to be back doing what she did best.

Jill sailed through the rest of her routine. There was nothing on her mind but her skating. By the time she came to the last jumps in her routine, she was relaxed and smiling. Jill performed the triple flip and double toe loop flawlessly and wound down gracefully to finish in a sit spin.

The music ended. Jill stood up and closed her eyes, making the moment last. She had skated well. She felt satisfied.

Jill glided off the ice and was greeted near the boards by the other Academy skaters and coaches.

"Nice job, Jill," Simon complimented her. "*Very* nice."

Jill caught Jesse's eye for a second. A big smile broke over his face. "Hi!" he mouthed. Jill smiled back, then turned away. She missed Jesse. She'd been so busy ignoring him, she forgot how good it felt to be nice to him.

Jill's scores were flashed on an electronic scoreboard. Simon put his arm around her and gave her a squeeze.

"Those are excellent scores, Jill," he said. "They're so close to Carla's that, off the top of my head, I can't figure out where that puts you."

Just then Jill heard a voice behind her. "Um, excuse me, you're Jill Wong, right?"

Jill turned and saw a little girl with blond braids, wearing a pink parka. The girl, who looked about eight, was sitting in a wheelchair and holding a notebook on her lap. A woman who looked as if she might be the girl's mother was standing nearby.

"Jill Wong?" the girl said again.

"Yes?" Jill regarded the girl curiously.

The little girl's face lit up. "It's me, Kim!"

"Kim?" Jill was confused.

"Kim, your Ice Pal!" the girl exclaimed.

"Kim, hi! What are you doing here?" Jill was amazed. She bent over to give the little girl a hug. "What about your operation?"

The woman beside Kim stepped forward. She put out her hand. "Hi, Jill. I'm Wendy Smalls, Kim's mother."

Jill shook Mrs. Smalls's hand. "It's nice to meet you."

"Kim's operation has been postponed. In fact, her leg muscles have gotten so strong, she might not even need an operation," Mrs. Smalls said, smiling down at Kim. She looked back at Jill. "Thank you so much for everything you've done for Kim."

"Me? But all I did was write Kim some letters," Jill said.

"Those letters made Kim's time in the hospital pass much faster." Mrs. Smalls beamed. "Kim loved hearing from you."

"I really liked getting *your* letters, too, Kim," Jill assured the little girl.

"I'm sorry I had to miss the Ice Pals show," Kim said. "I bet you were really good."

"Well, actually, I've skated better," Jill replied. "You didn't miss much. But I'm so glad you came today."

"Kim was so upset not to make it to the Ice Pals show," her mother explained. "She was doing so much better than everyone expected, the doctors released her from the hospital two days ago. But we couldn't make it to Kansas City in time for the show. Kim remembered reading in your letters that you'd be competing here today, so we thought we'd make the trip."

"Surprise!" Kim cried, laughing.

"What a great surprise," Jill said sincerely.

The little girl held out her notebook. "I brought my Dream Book for you to see! Look, here's your picture, right here." She opened the notebook.

Jill saw the picture she had sent Kim, the one Jill's little sister Randi had taken of Jill on the ice. Around the photograph a heart had been drawn in red marker.

"Wow," said Jill, touched.

"Do you think I could have your autograph underneath it?" Kim asked shyly.

"Well, sure," Jill answered. "If you want." She took the notebook. Kim's mother fished in her pocketbook and found a pen.

Jill thought a moment. Then she wrote, "To Kim, follow your own dreams. Love, your friend, Jill." She handed the notebook back to Kim.

"Oh, wow, thanks," Kim said sincerely. "This is the first real autograph I've ever gotten."

Jill laughed. "Well, I'm not exactly famous."

Kim's eyes were shining. "You will be, though, Jill. I just know it. And meeting you is the first dream in my Dream Book to come true. And the second one to come true is going to be when I take skating lessons from you."

Jill looked at Mrs. Smalls.

"Kim's doing better than the doctors ever could have hoped," Mrs. Smalls said, beaming.

"That's so great!" Jill said, squatting down next to Kim.

"The judges are about to announce the winners," Simon called from a few yards away.

"This is it," Jill said to Kim. "This is when I find out how I did."

"I think you were the best!" Kim said confidently. "They should give you first prize."

Jill grinned. "Thanks, Kim. I'm glad I have your vote."

Jill studied the board where the final standings would be posted. An announcer started calling the results.

Carla placed first. Jill felt a stab of disappointment. Even though she didn't want to compete against Carla any longer, it still hurt to lose. The announcer called out another name, and then he called Jill's name.

Kim tugged at the sleeve of Jill's skating dress. "Hey, Jill, that means you're third, right?"

Jill grinned. She had medaled after all!

"That's right, Kim," Jill answered with a smile.

"Third is pretty good, right?" Kim asked hopefully. "I mean, I know it's not first or anything, but it's pretty good, isn't it?"

"Yes," Jill agreed softly, looking down at Kim's smiling face. "It *is* pretty good."

17

Jill stood in line with the other skaters from the Academy, waiting to board the bus back to Denver. Alice David was there, chattering happily. Alice was one of the Academy kids who'd come to cheer her on at Sectionals.

"I can't believe that accident that you and Carla and Ludmila were in." Alice's eyes were wide. "Weren't you scared, Jill?"

"Sure," Jill responded. "But we knew we had to forget about being afraid and try to do something."

"It's so neat that you still made it to Sectionals in time to compete. I thought you did really well, Jill," Alice said with enthusiasm. "They definitely should have given you second, instead of third. You were better than that girl from Iowa or wherever, who placed second. Don't you think?"

Jill sighed. "I don't know, Alice. Anyway, I'm just happy I medaled."

The line of kids snaked forward toward the bus.

"Of course, Carla really did deserve to place first," Alice went on. "She was the best . . ." Alice paused. "Oops, sorry, Jill. I guess that wasn't so nice."

"That's okay, Alice," Jill answered truthfully. "You're right. Carla did skate well. Besides, for any good skater, the biggest competition should be with herself."

"I guess you're right," Alice commented as they approached the bus. "But coming in first must be a pretty good feeling."

Jill stepped up into the bus, with Alice close behind her.

"Oooh, there are Traci and Emily." Alice pointed. "I'm going to sit with them. You don't mind, right, Jill?"

"No, go ahead," Jill assured her. "I'm kind of tired anyway. I think I might take a nap on the way back. And Alice? Maybe this weekend I'll watch a video with you. Okay?"

Alice's eyes lit up. "Yeah! Okay!" The little girl took a seat across the aisle from her friends, and Jill made her way toward the back of the bus.

Then she spotted Jesse sitting a few rows back, next to the window. And sitting beside him was Carla!

I guess it's true, Jill thought. There's no chance left for Jesse and me.

Quickly she took a seat in an empty row. She gazed

out the window and watched the rest of the skaters board the bus.

Jill felt sad, but she realized that the best thing to do was to start learning to put Jesse and Carla out of her mind. After all, Jill couldn't *force* Jesse to like her better than he liked Carla. As Carla had said in the van right before the accident, Jill didn't *own* Jesse.

Besides, Jill told herself at last, if Jesse really wants to be with someone like Carla, he's probably not the right guy for me anyway.

Jill leaned her head back and shut her eyes.

The bus engine started, and someone sat down in the seat next to her. Jill turned to see who it was.

"Jesse!" she said, surprised.

"Is it okay if I sit here?" Jesse asked. "Or is this seat saved?"

"Of course it's okay," Jill answered. "I mean, if you want to."

"Of course I want to," Jesse responded. "And I'm glad I'm sitting on the outside. That way you can't run away."

"Run away?" Jill repeated.

"Yes, run away," Jesse said. "Like you do every time you see me lately. You're always rushing off somewhere. Or you're telling me how busy you are and *then* rushing off somewhere."

They sat in awkward silence for a moment. Questions flew through Jill's mind as she gazed out the window. Why did Jesse move over to sit with me? she wondered. Should I come right out and ask about him and Carla? Or should I still try to act like I'm not interested, like Veronica said?

"Look, Jill," Jesse said finally. "Why are you avoiding me?"

"What?" Jill said. "Avoiding you? What are you talking about?"

"Oh, come on," Jesse said. "You didn't say a single word to me at Sectionals. You made me feel like you didn't even care that I'd come to watch you compete."

"Really? You came to watch *me* compete?" Jill said in amazement.

Jesse grinned. "Who did you think I came to see? Carla?"

Jill lowered her eyes a moment. "Well, actually, yes."

"You're kidding!" Jesse was practically laughing. "Believe me, the last thing Carla needs is another admirer. She seems to be her own biggest fan already!"

Jill gaped at him. "But I thought you were taking her to the formal!" she blurted out.

"What?" Now Jesse was amazed.

"I thought you liked Carla!" Jill said.

"Sure, I liked Carla okay when I met her," he said. "I was trying to get along with her because she's *your* roommate. But when I got to know her better I realized she's kind of selfish."

"You did?" Jill asked.

"Yeah. Like she kept promising me she was going to help me with some problems I was having in math. But every time we got together to work, she just wanted to spend the whole time talking about the dance and how romantic it was going to be. I think maybe she was kind of hoping that I would ask her to go to the formal. But Carla's definitely not my type." He paused. "Besides, I already had someone I wanted to go to the formal with. Or I thought I did," he added softly.

Jill couldn't believe her ears. "You did?"

"Well, sure, Jill!" Jesse sounded frustrated. "I mean, I always kind of assumed that you and I would go together. And I figured you were thinking the same thing. But then after Carla arrived, you started acting all different, like you didn't care about me anymore."

"I can't believe this," Jill said. That's the last time I listen to any dumb magazine's advice about guys, she vowed silently.

"At first I thought it was just because you were busy with the Ice Pals project and getting ready for Sectionals," Jesse continued. "But I knew it had to be more than that. I couldn't figure out why you'd stopped being your regular friendly self around me."

"Oh, Jesse, I've been so dumb! I can't believe it!" Jill exclaimed. "You're right. I have been less friendly lately. But it was because I was convinced that you and Carla were getting closer. I was sure you liked Carla more than you liked me. At first I figured you and I would probably be going to the formal together, too. But after Carla came I got really worried that you were going to ask her instead."

"Now that *is* dumb!" Jesse joked.

Jill punched him lightly in the arm. "Hey! *I* can call myself dumb if I want, but you'd better not try it, Jesse!"

Jesse grinned and rubbed his arm. "Now that's the old Jill I remember!" He fixed his eyes on Jill. "So, what about it?"

"What about what?" Jill asked, teasing.

"The dance," Jesse responded. "Do we still have a date?"

Jill smiled. "Yes. We have a date."

And it's the old Jill Wong who's going with you to the dance, Jill added to herself. Because the old Jill Wong is back—for good!

**Don't miss any of the previous books in
the Silver Blades® series:**

#1: Breaking the Ice

Nikki Simon is thrilled when she makes the Silver Blades skating club. But Nikki quickly realizes that being a member of Silver Blades is going to be tougher than she thought. Both Nikki and another skater, Tori Carsen, have to land the double flip jump. But how far will Tori go to make sure *she* lands it first?

#2: In the Spotlight

Danielle Panati has always worked hard at her skating, and it's definitely starting to pay off. Danielle's just won the lead role in the Silver Blades Fall Ice Spectacular. Rehearsals go well at first; then the other members of Silver Blades start noticing that Danielle is acting strange. Is it the pressure of being in the spotlight—or does Danielle have a secret she doesn't want to share?

#3: The Competition

Tori Carsen loves skating when her mother isn't around, but as soon as her mother appears at the rink, skating becomes a nightmare. Mrs. Carsen argues with Tori's coaches and embarrasses her in front of the rest of the club. When Tori and several other members of Silver Blades go to Lake Placid for a regional competition, her mother becomes even more demanding. Could it have anything to do with a mysterious stranger who keeps showing up at the rink?

#4: Going for the Gold

It's a dream come true! Jill Wong is going to the famous figure-skating center in Colorado. But the training is *much* tougher than Jill ever expected, and Kevin, a really cute skater at the school, has a plan that's sure to get her into *big* trouble. Could this be the end of Jill's skating career?

#5: The Perfect Pair

Nikki Simon and Alex Beekman are the perfect pair on the ice. But off the ice there's a big problem. Suddenly Alex is sending Nikki gifts and asking her out on dates. Nikki wants to be Alex's partner in pairs but not his girlfriend. Will she lose Alex when she tells him? Can Nikki's friends in Silver Blades find a way to save her friendship with Alex *and* her skating career?

#6: Skating Camp

Summer's here and Jill can't wait to join her best friends from Silver Blades at skating camp. It's going to be just like old times. But things have changed since Jill left Silver Blades to train at a famous ice academy. Tori and Danielle are spending all their time with another skater, Haley Arthur, and Nikki has a big secret that she won't share with anyone. Has Jill lost her best friends forever?

#7: The Ice Princess

Tori's favorite skating superstar, Elyse Taylor, is in town, and she's staying with Tori! When Elyse promises to teach Tori her famous spin, Tori's sure they'll become the best of friends. But Elyse isn't the sweet champion everyone thinks she is. And she's going to make problems for Tori!

#8: Rumors at the Rink

Haley can't believe it—Kathy Bart, her favorite coach in the whole world, is quitting Silver Blades! Haley's sure it's all her fault. Why didn't she listen when everyone told her to stop playing practical jokes on Kathy? With Kathy gone, Haley knows she'll never win the next big competition. She has to make Kathy change her mind—no matter what. But will Haley's secret plan work?

#9: Spring Break

Jill is home from the Ice Academy, and everyone is treating her like a star. And she loves it! It's like a dream come true—especially when she meets cute, fifteen-year-old Ryan McKensey. He's so fun and cool—and he happens to be her number-one fan! The only problem is that he doesn't understand what it takes to be a professional athlete. Jill doesn't want to ruin her chances with such a great guy. But will dating Ryan destroy her future as an Olympic skater?

#10: Center Ice

It's gold medal time for Tori—she just knows it! The next big competition is coming up, and Tori has a winning routine. Now all she needs is that fabulous skating dress her mother promised her! But Mrs. Carsen doesn't seem to be interested in Tori's skating anymore—not since she started dating a new man in town. When Mrs. Carsen tells Tori she's not going to the competition, Tori decides enough is enough! She has a plan that will change everything—forever!

#11: A Surprise Twist

Danielle's on top of the world! All her hard work at the rink has paid off. She's good. Very good. And Dani's new English teacher, Ms. Howard, says she has a real flair for writing—she might even be the best writer in her class. Trouble is, there's a big skating competition coming up—*and* a writing contest. Dani's stumped. Her friends and family are counting on her to skate her best. But Ms. Howard is counting on her to write a winning story. How can Dani choose between skating and her new passion?

#12: The Winning Spirit

A group of Special Olympics skaters is on the way to Seneca Hills! The skaters are going to pair up with the Silver Blades members in a mini-competition. Everyone in Silver Blades thinks Nikki Simon is really lucky—her Special Olympics partner is Carrie, a girl with Down syndrome who's one of the best visiting skaters. But Nikki can't seem to warm up to the idea of skating with Carrie. In fact, she seems to be hiding something . . . but what?

#13: The Big Audition

Holiday excitement is in the air! Jill Wong, one of the best skaters in Silver Blades, is certain she will win the leading role of Clara in the *Nutcracker on Ice* spectacular. Until young skater Amber Armstrong comes along. At first Jill can't believe that Amber is serious competition. But she had better believe it—and fast! Because she's about to find herself completely out of the spotlight.

#14: Nutcracker on Ice

Nothing is going Jill Wong's way. She hates her role in the *Nutcracker on Ice* spectacular. And she's hardly on the ice long enough to be noticed! To top it all off, the Ice Academy coaches seem awfully impressed with Jill's main rival, Amber Armstrong. Jill has worked so hard to return to the Academy, and now she might lose her chance. Does Jill have what it takes to save her lifelong dream?

Super Edition #1: Rinkside Romance

Tori, Haley, Nikki, and Amber are at the Junior Nationals, where a figure skater's dreams can really come true! But Amber's trying too hard, and her skating is awful. Tori's in trouble with an important judge. Nikki and Alex are fighting so much they might not make it into the competition. And someone is sending them all mysterious love notes! Are their skating dreams about to turn into nightmares?

#15: A New Move

Haley's got a big problem. Lately her parents have been fighting more than ever. And now her dad is moving out—and going to live in Canada! Haley just doesn't see how she can live without him. Especially since the only thing her mom and sister ever talk about is her sister's riding. They don't care about Haley's skating at all! There's one clever move that could solve all Haley's problems. Does she have the nerve to go through with it?

#16: Ice Magic

Martina Nemo has always dreamed of skating in the Ice Capades. So when she lands a skating role in a television movie, it seems too good to be true! Martina loves to perform in front of the camera. It's a lot of fun—especially when all her friends in Silver Blades visit her on the set to cheer her on. Then Martina discovers something terrible: Someone is out to ruin her chance of a lifetime. . . .

#17: A Leap Ahead

Amber Armstrong is only eleven, but she can already skate as well as—even better than—the older girls in Silver Blades. The only problem is that the other skaters still treat her like a baby. So Amber decides to take the senior-level skating test. She'll be the youngest skater ever to pass, and then the other girls will *have* to stop treating her like a little kid. Amber is sure her plan will work. But is she headed for success or for total disaster?

#18: More Than Friends

Nikki's furious. Her skating partner, Alex, and her good friend, Haley, are dating each other. Nikki knows she shouldn't be jealous, but she is. She'd do anything to break them up. And she knows how to do it, too. But should she? Or will Nikki end up with no friends at all?

Super Edition #2: Wedding Secrets

It's happening! Tori's mom is getting married! Everything has to be perfect—the invitations, the bridesmaids' dresses, and especially Tori's big wedding surprise. No problem! Tori has it all under control. Until she gets a surprise of her own—a new stepsister, Veronica! Suddenly Veronica starts giving orders, and everyone's listening to *her*. Tori is steaming mad. But she knows Veronica is hiding something big. And Tori's going to find out what it is—before Veronica takes over the wedding, and the rest of Tori's life!

#19: Natalia Comes to America

Russian figure skater Natalia Cherkas has dreamed all her life of skating in America—and now her dream has come true! She's moving in with Tori Carsen's family and joining Silver Blades. But as soon as Natalia arrives, her dream turns into a nightmare. The girls in Silver Blades don't want to be her friends. She can't work with her new coach. And she's horribly homesick. Natalia wants to return to Russia—now! So she comes up with a secret plan to run away. There's just one problem. Natalia needs Tori's help—and getting it is not going to be easy!

#20: The Only Way to Win

Amber Armstrong will have to quit figure skating! Her parents say her skating lessons are too expensive. Then Isabel Hart shows up. Isabel wants to sponsor Amber—she'll pay for all her lessons and even buy her a new skating wardrobe! Isabel promises Amber that together they'll make her into a winner. Amber is really happy until she discovers the horrifying truth. Isabel will do anything—including bribing the judges—to help Amber get ahead. Now Amber must decide how important winning really is!

DO YOU HAVE A YOUNGER BROTHER OR SISTER?

Maybe he or she would like to meet Jill Wong's little sister Randi and her friends in the exciting new series

SILVER BLADES®
FIGURE EIGHTS

Look for these titles at your bookstore or library:

ICE DREAMS
STAR FOR A DAY
THE BEST ICE SHOW EVER!
BOSSY ANNA
DOUBLE BIRTHDAY TROUBLE
SPECIAL DELIVERY MESS
RANDI'S MISSING SKATES
MY WORST FRIEND, WOODY
And coming soon:
RANDI'S PET SURPRISE

LEARN TO SKATE!

SKATE WITH U.S.
A SPECIAL PROGRAM FOR BEGINNERS

WHAT IS **SKATE WITH U.S.?**

Designed by the United States Figure Skating Association (USFSA) and sponsored by the United States Postal Service, Skate With U.S. is a beginning ice-skating program that is fun, challenging, and rewarding. Skaters of all ages are welcome!

HOW DO I JOIN **SKATE WITH U.S.?**

Skate With U.S. is offered at many rinks and clubs across the country. Contact your local rink or club to see if it offers the USFSA Basic Skills program. Or **call 1-800-269-0166** for more information about the Skate With U.S. program in your area.

WHAT DO I GET WHEN I JOIN **SKATE WITH U.S.?**

When you join Skate With U.S. through a club or a rink, you will be registered as an official USFSA Basic Skills Member, and you will receive:

- Official Basic Skills Membership Card
- Basic Skills Record Book with stickers
- Official Basic Skills member patch
- Year patch, denoting membership year
  And much, much more!

PLUS you may be eligible to participate in a "Compete With U.S." competition hosted by sponsoring clubs and rinks!

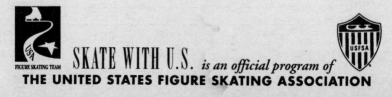

SKATE WITH U.S. *is an official program of*
THE UNITED STATES FIGURE SKATING ASSOCIATION

A FAN CLUB—JUST FOR YOU!
JOIN THE USA FIGURE SKATING INSIDE TICKET FAN CLUB!

As a member of this special skating fan club, you get:

- **Six issues of SKATING MAGAZINE!**
  For the inside edge on what's happening on and off the ice!

- **Your very own copy of MAGIC MEMORIES ON ICE!**
  A 90-minute video produced by ABC Sports featuring the world's greatest skaters!

- **An Official USA FIGURE SKATING TEAM Pin!**
  Available only to Inside Ticket Fan Club members!

- **A limited-edition photo of the U.S. World Figure Skating Team!**
  Available only to Inside Ticket Fan Club members!

- **The Official USA FIGURE SKATING INSIDE TICKET Membership Card!** For special discounts on USA Figure Skating collectibles and memorabilia!

To join the USA FIGURE SKATING INSIDE TICKET Fan Club, fill out the form below and send it with $24.95, plus $3.95 for shipping and handling (U.S. funds only, please!), to:

> Sports Fan Network
> USA Figure Skating Inside Ticket
> P.O. Box 581
> Portland, Oregon 97207-0581

Or call the Sports Fan Network membership hotline at **1-800-363-8796!**

NAME:_____

ADDRESS:_____

CITY:_____ **STATE:**_____ **ZIP:**_____

PHONE: (____)_____DATE OF BIRTH:_____